Wind
A No

Wind Shear: A Novella

Ann Marie Spencer

Published by Ann Marie Spencer, 2024.

This is a work of fiction. Similarities to real people, places, or events are entirely coincidental.

WIND SHEAR: A NOVELLA

First edition. November 15, 2024.

Copyright © 2024 Ann Marie Spencer.

ISBN: 979-8227431899

Written by Ann Marie Spencer.

To Being A SIGMA INFJ

You'll begin again, and you'll end again—many times.

Yet through it all, life continues its steady forward march.

CHAPTER 1

The college town buzzed with an uncontrollable energy, its sun-drenched streets alive with the constant motion of youth and ambition. The air hummed with the whir of bicycle wheels and the steady thrum of footsteps on cracked sidewalks. Students with backpacks slung over their shoulders mingled with professionals clutching coffee cups, all moving with the purposeful gait of those with places to be and dreams to chase.

Amid this carefully choreographed chaos, an expensive car—sleek, black, and jarringly out of place—screeched to a sudden halt to double-park with an air of entitlement. The abrupt stop sent a ripple of disruption through the flow of pedestrians and cyclists, drawing curious and annoyed glances alike.

From the passenger side emerged Jayde Masipang-Rivera, a poised twenty-five-year-old Filipina whose presence commanded attention. Her long, dark hair, usually perfectly styled, was disheveled from the heated argument that had raged inside the car. Her eyes, typically warm and inviting, now flashed with a fury that charged the air around her. With a forceful slam of the door, she exited—a physical punctuation to the words she had hurled moments before.

"You're crazy, Jayde!" rang out of the driver's side, where Cesaro leaned out of the window. In his mid-twenties as well, Cesaro's dark

Latino features twisted in rage, a striking contrast to his designer attire. The polished exterior he typically presented to the world crumbled, revealing raw emotion beneath.

Jayde spun around, her hair catching the sunlight as it whipped in the wind. The movement was graceful, almost balletic, but her words sliced through the air with cutting precision. "Enough! I'm sick of this!" Her voice conveyed both disgust and resolve—the culmination of too many unendurable moments.

Sensing the finality in her tone, Cesaro scrambled out of the car, leaving the driver's door ajar, further obstructing pedestrians and motorists. "Get back here!" he demanded, his voice a discordant blend of anger and desperation. "We're not done, Jayde!"

But Jayde was done. In one swift motion, she yanked the engagement ring from her finger. The diamond, once a symbol of love and promise, now felt cold and burdensome. With all the strength her anger lent her, she threw it hard at Cesaro's car. The tiny stone caught the sunlight as it arced through the air, a fleeting symbol of dreams now tossed in the wind, glinting one last time before vanishing from sight.

"Yes, we are!" Jayde's voice had the weight and finality of a judge's gavel. "The engagement is off. I'm done, Cesaro. We're not getting married." Each word was deliberate, leaving no room for misinterpretation.

Cesaro's expression shifted, disbelief giving way to anger. He scoffed, venom lacing his voice in a way he had never willingly shown before. The reality of the situation began to sink in. "Stop playing," he said, his voice losing its edge. "Jayde! You'll be back!"

But Jayde walked away, her heels clicking against the pavement in sync with her racing heart. Every step carried her farther from

Cesaro and closer to a future she could not yet envision. Entering the apartment building, she climbed the stairs swiftly, eager to escape the scene she had just left behind.

When Jayde reached her apartment, number 331, her hands shook so badly that she struggled to fit the key into the lock. The metal trembled against the keyhole, scraping the side with a harsh, grating sound. After a few fumbling moments, a quiet click signaled her success, and the door swung open.

She stumbled inside, slamming the door shut with the same force she had used moments earlier to leave the car. The resounding bang echoed through the apartment, mirroring the storm of emotions raging within her. Her heart pounded in her chest; each beat was a painful reminder of the decision she had just made.

With unsteady steps, Jayde made her way to her bedroom, her sanctuary. As she crossed the threshold, the adrenaline coursing through her veins began to ebb, leaving her hollow and drained.

Unable to stand any longer, she collapsed onto her bed. The soft mattress seemed to swallow her as she instinctively sought refuge from the emotional onslaught. In the stillness of the room, the first sob escaped her lips—raw and painful. It was as though a dam had burst, and suddenly, she could not stop the flood of tears.

The familiar surroundings of her room, once a source of comfort, now seemed to mock her with memories of happier times. Her eyes landed on a photograph perched on her nightstand. The image of Cesaro, his face split by a wide, carefree smile, seemed to taunt her. That smile, once a source of joy and security, now felt like a cruel haunt.

Half in anguish, half in rage, Jayde seized the frame. With a strangled cry, she hurled it across the room. The satisfying sound of shattering glass filled the air as the frame struck the opposite wall. The crash was oddly cathartic, giving physical form to the dissolution of their relationship.

Jayde stared at the bare wall where the photo had struck, her mind a maelstrom of conflicting emotions. How had it come to this? Just a week ago, she had been giddy with excitement, her future seemingly set in stone. But now, here she was, surrounded by the broken shards of that dream. The bare wall became a blank canvas, once so clearly filled with her future. The oppressive silence of the room was broken only by her ragged breathing and the occasional sobs.

A few days later, Jayde found herself in a quaint coffee shop, sitting across from her reserved, sandy-haired friend, Hannah, who was also in her mid-twenties. The familiar setting felt surreal as if she had stepped into a scene from her old life. Both women were casually dressed, but the underlying tension between them was palpable.

Hannah sipped a cold, fruity concoction, the cheerful drink at odds with the somber atmosphere. Jayde cradled a steaming cup of coffee, its bitter aroma matching her mood. She could feel Hannah's concerned gaze on her, but Jayde couldn't bring herself to meet it. Her eyes darted around, taking in the bustling café—the echo of laughter, the clinking of cups, and the sunlight streaming through the windows, casting a warm glow on everything. Yet, inside, she felt enveloped in shadow, the vibrant colors around her muted by the storm brewing within her heart.

The silence between them grew more uncomfortable with each passing second. Jayde knew she should say something, but the words seemed lodged in her throat. How could she possibly explain the upheaval of the past week?

Unable to bear the tension any longer, Jayde finally broke the silence with a sigh. "It's been a hell of a week," she said, her voice hoarse from disuse. She paused, steeling herself. "I finally broke it off with Cesaro."

The words hung heavy in the air between them. Jayde watched as Hannah's eyes widened, clearly surprised by the sudden announcement.

"Um... Really?" Hannah's reply was slow hesitant, her voice full of question marks. "Jayde, are you sure? It feels so sudden."

Jayde shrugged, trying to affect an air of nonchalance that she didn't feel. Inside, she was a mess, but she was determined not to show it. "It was easier than I thought." The words left a bitter taste in her mouth.

Desperate to steer the conversation away from the wreckage of her personal life, Jayde seized the first topic that came to mind. "Anyway, I think I've finally found a subject for my final project."

As Hannah asked about the project, Jayde felt a flicker of excitement. This was something she could focus on—something separate from the tangled emotions of her relationship. She latched onto it with relief, explaining about the CEO she had found through a connection with her uncle.

But even as she spoke, she couldn't ignore the awkward pauses in their conversation or the way Hannah carefully chose her words. Their once easy friendship now felt fragile, as if it had been replaced by something more tentative.

The conversation stumbled along, and both women were unsure of how to navigate the delicate terrain their relationship had become. When Hannah mistakenly referred to them both as writing majors, Jayde's correction came out sharper than she intended. "We are NOT both writing majors... YOU are. I'm a JOURNALISM major."

She immediately regretted the harshness in her tone but couldn't stop herself. It was as if all the pain and frustration of the past week came bubbling to the surface.

When Hannah brought up Cesaro again, Jayde felt her defenses flare. "Hannah, let's not pretend you've been a great friend when it comes to Cesaro," she snapped, instantly regretting the words. She knew she was being unfair, and she knew Hannah was only trying to help, but the flood of emotions was too strong to contain.

Before Hannah could respond, Jayde's phone rang, startling them both. She glanced at the screen, a mix of relief and apprehension crossing her face. "It's Aunt Cassidy," she said, answering Hannah's questioning look.

As Jayde picked up the call, a cacophony of voices on the other end immediately drew her attention, a sharp contrast to the quiet tension of the café.

"Can you hear me?" she asked, raising her voice slightly. "What on earth is happening over there?"

Cassidy Valencia, standing in the middle of a corporate whirlwind, looked as composed as ever in her tailored suit. Despite juggling the phone and a pile of multiplying documents, Jayde's forty-five-year-old aunt remained poised. As Cassidy explained the crisis at work, Jayde felt a familiar knot forming in her stomach. She knew where this conversation was heading, already sensing the weight of familial obligation settling on her shoulders once again.

When Cassidy asked her to pick up the kids from school, Jayde hesitated, a sigh slipping through her lips. She glanced at Hannah, who was watching her with thinly veiled curiosity.

"Jayde!" Cassidy's sharp tone snapped her back to attention.

"No—I mean, yes, of course. I'll do it," Jayde stammered, resigned.

"I'll see you tonight. Love you," Cassidy said, her tone softening slightly.

"Love you, too," Jayde replied, ending the call. She turned to Hannah, her shoulders slumping. "I have to pick up my brother and sister from school. There go my plans for the day."

Hannah frowned. "Do you really have to? Robin's sixteen, and there are plenty of buses. Shouldn't she be learning to be independent by now? She could easily get Felipe home."

Jayde snorted, a mix of amusement and frustration. "You know how my family is..." She trailed off, not needing to explain further. Hannah had witnessed the complexities of Jayde's family dynamics too many times.

"It's a shame you don't have more freedom," Hannah mused, stirring her drink absently. "You're always dropping everything."

"I wouldn't know what freedom feels like, anyway," Jayde muttered, her voice tinged with bitterness. The words hung between them, heavy with unspoken resentment.

Hannah's eyes lit up as if struck by sudden inspiration. "Someone once said... it's about becoming someone we never thought we'd be."

Jayde rolled her eyes, not in the mood for philosophical musings. "Well, I never imagined I'd be a chauffeur for a preteen and a teenager, so clearly, the lack of freedom has the same effect."

"I don't think that's what it means—" Hannah began, but Jayde cut her off.

"Forget it. I have to go. They're probably waiting already." Jayde stood, gathering her things. She paused, her expression softening. Despite the tension, she knew Hannah was only trying to help. "Just stop asking me about Cesaro. You know it's a sensitive subject for us."

Hannah nodded, a flicker of guilt crossing her face. "Yeah, I know. I just wish things could go back to the way they were."

As Jayde walked away, leaving Hannah behind at the café, she echoed the sentiment. She, too, wished things could return to the way they were—before the breakup, before the arguments with Cesaro, before her family's demands became so overwhelming. But as she slid into her car, ready to pick up her siblings, she knew it wasn't possible. She glanced in the rearview mirror, catching a glimpse of Hannah still sitting at the table, lost in thought.

The drive to the school was short, but for Jayde, it felt like an eternity. Her mind raced, replaying the argument with Cesaro, the unfinished project looming over her, and the constant responsibilities pressing down on her. As she pulled up to the curb, she spotted her siblings waiting—each standing in a way that perfectly reflected their personalities.

Felipe, her twelve-year-old brother, stood quietly, clutching his backpack to his chest like a shield. His wide, observant eyes seemed to take in everything around him. Robin, on the other hand, radiated teenage irritation, her crossed arms and scowling face a clear warning to all.

As Robin slid into the front passenger seat, Jayde could almost feel the waves of annoyance emanating from her sister. "Why are

YOU here?" Robin demanded, not even sparing a glance at Jayde, and her gaze fixed out the window.

Jayde gripped the steering wheel tighter, her knuckles whitening as she forced herself to stay calm. She'd already faced one emotional confrontation today; she didn't need another. "Tiya had to stay late at work," she explained, keeping her voice even. "Some kind of accounting error."

"And what about Tiyo Logan?" Robin pressed, her tone teetering on the edge of provoking a fight.

Jayde felt her patience fraying. It had been a long day, and it wasn't even halfway over. "Robin, I don't know," she snapped, immediately regretting the sharpness in her voice. She took a deep breath before continuing, "Tiya asked me to pick you guys up. That's all I know."

As they pulled away from the school, Jayde glanced in the rearview mirror, meeting Felipe's eyes. Her younger brother had always been the quiet one, more prone to observing than speaking. But now, he leaned forward, his voice small and hesitant. "Ate... What about Ma?"

The air in the car seemed to thicken, tension settling around them. Jayde's heart sank at the mention of their mother. She glanced at Robin, who had gone stiff in her seat, a frown deepening on her face.

"Ma's fine," Jayde said, forcing a smile that felt fragile. "She's just busy with work right now."

Even as she spoke, she could feel the weight of her words, like a thin veneer barely holding together the illusion of normalcy. She hoped it would be enough to ease their worries, but deep down, she knew they couldn't avoid the truth forever.

The silence that followed was heavy with unspoken emotions. Jayde's mind raced, remembering all the times their mother had let them down, all the broken promises and missed moments. Before she could say more, Robin scoffed, her voice laced with bitterness. "Forget her! Nobody cares where she is."

Jayde glanced in the mirror and saw Felipe shrink back into his seat, his shoulders slumping. His quiet, almost whispered, "...I care," cut through her like a blade.

She inhaled deeply, searching for the right words. How could she explain their mother's absence without shattering Felipe's hope or fueling Robin's anger? "I don't know where she is," she said softly. "I haven't heard from her, and neither has Tiya or Tiyo. So you just have to make do with me."

"I didn't mean it like that!" Felipe's voice was a rushed plea. "You just...You're always there for us, just like a Ma. But you shouldn't have to do that. That's Ma's job."

A lump formed in Jayde's throat. She'd never asked for this responsibility, never wanted to be a stand-in parent for her siblings. But here she was, doing her best in a role she hadn't chosen.

To her surprise, it was Robin who spoke next, her voice softer than Jayde had heard in months. "Hey... Jayde's our big sister, right? Our Ate." She paused as if considering her next words carefully. "And that's even better because we can tell her anything without getting into trouble."

"Almost anything," Felipe chimed in, a hint of mischief flickering in his voice.

Jayde chuckled despite herself, the tension in the car easing just a bit. She caught Robin's eye, and they shared a brief, knowing smile. The weight of her responsibilities still pressed heavily on her, but at that moment, Jayde felt a surge of love for her siblings.

They were a family, for better or worse, navigating life's challenges together.

CHAPTER 2

A day later, Jayde wandered through the local park, her mind still a whirlwind of unresolved emotions. The sun beat down on the path lined with benches, warming the skin of the few patrons enjoying the afternoon. Jayde paced back and forth, her phone pressed to her ear as she tried yet again to reach someone.

"The number you have dialed is currently unavail—" The automated voice cut off abruptly as Jayde ended the call with a frustrated huff, running her free hand through her hair.

Pausing near the sidewalk, her gaze settled on two women seated on a nearby bench. The older of the two, a white woman who looked to be in her early eighties, glanced at Jayde with mild annoyance. Beside her sat a black woman, likely in her early forties, dressed in white nursing scrubs embroidered with NERINE ASSISTED LIVING, CHARLOTTE. The aide seemed oblivious to Jayde's presence, absorbed in a puzzle book.

Before Jayde could ponder the pair further, a sudden commotion erupted nearby, startling the trio. Their heads turned in unison toward the source.

"No! I've changed my mind! I can't!"

At the end of the path where it met the main road, a young mother—barely out of her teens—stood beside a pile of trash bags.

In her arms, she cradled a wailing baby, their cries creating a heart-wrenching duet.

A spry older woman rushed up to the young mother, her face twisted in fury. "Give me my grandchild!" she demanded, her voice ringing out like a clarion call. "Get your life together, Marissa. Grow up a little, and then we'll see if you're ready to be a mother."

The girl burst into tears again, her face falling as she nodded and began to gather the child's belongings. The grandmother continued, "I'll take her now. Don't trouble yourself; I have everything she needs." At that moment, the young mother tearfully surrendered the baby, relinquishing not just her child but perhaps a piece of her soul.

Jayde watched the scene unfold, a knot forming in her stomach. The young mother's sobs, the grandmother's stern admonitions, the baby's cries—it all merged into a chaotic symphony of family pain, laid bare for the world to see.

As the grandmother drove away with the baby, the young mother stood frozen, ashen and alone. She gathered her bags and slowly made her way across the park, a hollow figure adrift.

A storm of emotions swirled within Jayde, creating an internal tempest she couldn't quite placate. Part of her wanted to look away, to pretend she hadn't witnessed this private moment of anguish. Yet another part couldn't help but judge.

"That's such a shame," Charlotte murmured, clicking her tongue.

The older woman beside her nodded sagely. "That young girl is brave."

Jayde couldn't hide her disbelief and let out a snort, drawing their attention. "Brave? It's selfish to have a child you can't take care of."

The older woman's eyes narrowed, a spark of defiance in her gaze. "She's trying. Look at those bags—they're probably filled with the baby's things."

"What good is trying if she's failing so miserably, Mrs...?" Jayde retorted, her tone sharp.

"No, 'Mrs.' Just call me Eleanor. Or don't call me at all if you can't understand that trying takes more courage than most people have."

Jayde bristled at the rebuke. "Surely, she had plenty of opportunities to... do something else."

"I certainly did," Eleanor replied, her voice distant, as if recalling another time.

"Did what?" Jayde found herself asking, curiosity overriding her irritation.

Eleanor's gaze returned to Jayde, a hint of reminiscent displacement lingering in her eyes. "Chose... 'something else.' I commend that mother for even having her child. I was not strong enough."

There was something in Eleanor's tone that made Jayde pause. Without realizing it, she moved closer, sitting beside the older woman. "What do you mean?"

Eleanor sighed, her eyes once again taking on a distant look, drifting back to that far-off place. "I wasn't much older than that girl. I got pregnant and told no one—not even the father." She paused as if the memory had grown heavy with time. "I remember my clothes weren't quite fitting, so I had a feeling that I might be. I never kept track of my monthlies, but I just expected it. This time, however, it felt off. So, I took a test."

As Eleanor spoke, the sounds of the bustling park faded into the background. Jayde was drawn into her story, picturing a young

Eleanor standing at a crossroads with a choice that would change her life forever...

———⁂———

The warm water cascaded over Eleanor's trembling form as she cowered in the shower. At nineteen, she should have been excited—on the cusp of adulthood, ready to take on the world. Instead, she felt small, vulnerable, and utterly terrified. Her hands moved to her abdomen, still flat, yet harboring a secret that threatened to upend her entire life.

"What do I do?" she whispered, her voice barely audible over the running water. "No one can know..."

Eleanor's mind raced, struggling to grasp the limited options before her as she fought to hold back tears. Legally, she was an adult, but the decision that lay ahead made her feel anything but. With shaking hands, she turned off the water and stepped out, going through the motions of drying off and dressing, each movement mechanical, detached.

"I was fortunate enough to get an appointment with my gynecologist for the next day."

The gynecologist's office was in polarity to Eleanor's inner turmoil. Cheerful posters filled the walls, showcasing smiling babies and glowing mothers-to-be. Knick-knacks celebrating the miracle of life cluttered every surface. Eleanor felt like an imposter in this shrine to motherhood.

The doctor, a middle-aged man with a perpetual smile, beamed at her from across his desk. "Congratulations!" he exclaimed, his voice dripping with well-practiced enthusiasm.

Eleanor's eyes widened, her breath catching in her throat. The cheerful room fell into an awkward silence as the doctor read something in her expression. Clearing his throat, his demeanor shifted to something more serious.

"Do you intend to continue the pregnancy?" he asked gently.

Her response came as barely a whisper. "No."

The doctor nodded, his voice becoming more clinical. "I can schedule an appointment for you... for termination if that's your decision."

Eleanor nodded, unable to speak. As she agreed, it felt as though she were watching herself from outside her own body, detached from the moment, making a decision that would change her life forever.

Back in the present, Eleanor's voice had softened. "And so, it was done," she murmured, her eyes fixed on something far beyond the park pond in front of them.

Jayde leaned in, captivated by Eleanor's unbridled retelling. "Then what happened?" she urged.

Eleanor sighed—a lifetime of complex emotions wrapped in a single breath. "I felt numb, yet relieved. It wasn't until a year later that I truly reacted to what I had done."

"How did you react?" Jayde asked, her journalistic instincts stirring despite her emotional investment in the story.

A wry smile played at the corners of Eleanor's mouth. "I unleashed a verbal assault on my boyfriend, who had only just heard of it. He listened, never interrupting, and quietly said, 'I'm sorry,' then held me until all my high emotions dissipated." As she finished, the sounds of the park rushed back in.

Charlotte rummaged loudly through her oversized purse, shattering the moment's spell. Eleanor shot her a look of annoyance as Charlotte triumphantly pulled out a lip balm, ignoring their irritated glances.

Eleanor sighed, her gaze drifting back to the pond where ducks glided across the water, bathed in the golden light of the setting sun. The weight of the past seemed to hang heavily over them.

Jayde opened her mouth to ask one of the many questions swirling in her mind, but she was interrupted by the shrill ring of her phone. Excusing herself, she stepped away to answer the call, feeling as though she were being yanked from one world into another, Eleanor's poignant memories fading like a vivid dream upon waking. Her heart sank as she recognized the number—it was the CEO she was hoping to interview for her project.

"Jayde, I'm afraid I have to cancel our meeting," the CEO's voice came through, abrupt and unapologetic.

"But, sir, we had an agreement. This interview is crucial for my project," Jayde protested, her free hand clenching into a fist.

"My time is very valuable," he replied dismissively. "I have a magazine interview in a few minutes. If you want to reschedule, talk to my secretary. She'll give you a quote for the interview."

Jayde's face flushed with frustration. "You said this meeting was a favor to my uncle. Is this how you treat all your business associates?"

There was a pause before the CEO spoke again, his tone condescending. "Listen, kid, you've got to get used to this. This is how the industry works."

"Great. Thanks for the lesson," Jayde bit out, ending the call before she said something she would regret. She stood for a moment, phone clutched tightly in her hand, trying to calm her racing thoughts.

As her frustration simmered, Jayde's gaze returned to Eleanor and Charlotte on the bench. A spark of inspiration ignited. Maybe this setback was an opportunity.

Taking a deep breath to steady herself, Jayde strode back to the bench, a new determination in her step. Eleanor eyed her approach with suspicion and annoyance.

"What are you doing?" Eleanor asked, her voice sharp with irritation.

Jayde sat down, her posture relaxed but her eyes bright with purpose. "I was just sitting here," she said lightly. "Anyway, I have a favor to ask."

Eleanor's eyebrow arched skeptically, her weathered face betraying distrust. "What?"

"I'm a journalism major," Jayde explained, leaning forward with marked enthusiasm. "And for my final project, I need to write a biographical account of someone interesting. Someone real and present."

"So? What does that have to do with me?" Eleanor retorted, sarcasm dripping from her voice.

Undeterred, Jayde pressed on. "Your story was quite interesting. I'd like to meet with you to have an interview about your life."

"No," Eleanor said flatly.

"Why not?" Jayde asked, refusing to back down.

Eleanor's eyes flashed with irritation. "You bother me."

Jayde's expression softened. "How? Don't you want your legacy to be remembered?"

A flicker of something—regret, maybe fear—crossed Eleanor's face before she masked it with a scowl. "Nobody cares about me. Besides, I don't have anything worth remembering."

"I think stories like yours could help others," Jayde insisted earnestly. "What if that young mother heard your story?"

Eleanor's eyes narrowed. "Why? Are you going to tell her?"

"Eleanor..." Jayde began, but the older woman cut her off with a wave of her hand.

"Ugh. I forgot I told you my name."

At that moment, Charlotte stood up, her smile apologetic as she addressed Jayde. "I'm sorry, dear. We have to go. The home keeps its residents on a tight schedule."

Jayde nodded slowly, her gaze lingering on the logo stitched on Charlotte's scrubs. The sight only strengthened her resolve.

"Come on, Miss Eleanor. Time to go," Charlotte said gently, helping Eleanor to her feet.

"I told you to just call me Eleanor!" the older woman grumbled, though her tone had lost some of its edge.

As Jayde watched them walk toward the nursing home vehicle, her mind was already whirring with plans. The setback with the CEO might have been the push she needed to pursue a far more compelling—and far more human—story than she'd originally imagined.

The next day, Jayde found herself standing in the quiet, cozy lobby of Nerine Assisted Living. The soft hum of conversation and rustling papers created a soothing atmosphere, belying the nervous energy coursing through her. She approached the reception desk, her heart pounding.

"Hello, I'm here to see my aunt," Jayde said, trying to keep her voice steady.

The receptionist looked up, her face a mask of professional politeness. "Good morning. What's your name?"

Jayde took a deep breath, preparing herself for the lie. "I'm Miss Eleanor's niece, Jayde Masipang-Rivera."

The receptionist's eyebrows rose slightly as she glanced at Jayde's distinctive Filipino features. Jayde felt a bead of sweat on her brow.

"I'm adopted," she added quickly, congratulating herself on her quick thinking.

Before the receptionist could respond, a familiar voice rang out. Jayde turned to see Charlotte entering the lobby, her white scrubs crisp and pristine.

"Good morning, dear," Charlotte greeted, her eyes widening in surprise. "What are you doing here?"

Jayde gently pulled her aside, lowering her voice. "I've been thinking a lot about Eleanor," she confessed. "She's quite an interesting person, and I'd love to continue our conversation."

Charlotte's expression softened, a knowing smile forming. "I think talking to you was good for her," she said. "She can be prickly, but I think she was a bit more pleased to speak to you than she let on. She's like that sometimes."

Jayde nodded eagerly. "I believe it."

"Well, I'm off to see her now," Charlotte said with a wink. "I hope things work out for you. Maybe I'll see you around."

"I'll see you soon," Jayde replied, determination in her voice.

As Charlotte made her way to Eleanor's room, Jayde turned back to the receptionist, a confident smile on her face.

"Charlotte and I met yesterday when I was visiting my... aunt," she coolly explained.

The receptionist nodded, satisfied. "Of course. ID, please, and just sign in here."

Jayde signed her name, asking casually, "Could you remind me what room my aunt is in?"

"Down that hallway, then make a left," the receptionist replied. "It's about mid-way down. Room 4212."

"Thank you so much!" Jayde said, her voice warm with gratitude.

With one last smile at the receptionist, Jayde made her way down the hallway, her heart racing with a mixture of excitement and trepidation. She was one step closer to her goal, but the hardest part was still ahead. As she neared Eleanor's room, Jayde took a deep breath, preparing for what was to come. Whatever happened next, she knew it would be a turning point for her project.

Jayde knocked gently on the open door of Eleanor's room, poking her head around the corner. The scene before her was one of domestic tranquility: Eleanor sat in a chair at a small round table while Charlotte busied herself making the bed. Both women looked up in surprise at Jayde's entrance.

Eleanor's eyes narrowed as she recognized her visitor. "How the hell did you find me?" she demanded, her voice a mix of annoyance and grudging admiration.

Jayde grinned, emboldened by her success. "Well, 'AUNTIE,' it's visiting hours for family right now," she replied, stressing the word with a hint of mischief.

Eleanor's face darkened. "You clever little brat," she growled. "Charlotte! Get her out of here."

Charlotte hesitated, glancing between the two women. Jayde seized her moment. "I'll make a deal with you," she said quickly. "If you agree to be my subject for the project."

"I said no," Eleanor snapped. "Charlotte!"

As Charlotte moved to help Eleanor put on a cardigan, Jayde pressed on, her words tumbling out in a rush. "I'll take you to the park so you and Charlotte can have a break. I noticed you two were getting on each other's nerves the other day."

A flicker of amusement crossed Eleanor's face. "Very astute," she muttered.

Encouraged, Jayde continued, "If you come with me, I'll take you wherever you want to go. You'll tell me about your life, and you get to pick the topics."

Eleanor scoffed, but Jayde noticed a flicker of interest in her eyes. "Oh, please. I'll be dead soon, anyway. You probably won't even get to finish your project."

"Don't say that, Eleanor!" Charlotte gently admonished.

Jayde leaned in, her voice low and determined. "Okay. If you're going to be dead before I'm done, what do you care if people know about your life or not?"

A heavy silence fell over the room. Jayde held her breath, watching emotions flicker across Eleanor's face. Charlotte suppressed a smile, amused by the standoff.

Finally, Eleanor let out a loud laugh that startled both Jayde and Charlotte. "You cheeky little girl!" she exclaimed, shaking her head. "Fine. Only because I appreciate your tenacity, but remember, I choose what stories to tell. And if I want to stop at any point, we stop. Understood?"

Jayde nodded eagerly, barely believing in her success. "Anything you want," she agreed quickly. "I'll let you talk, and I won't ask for a specific story."

Eleanor's eyes narrowed, considering the offer. "Fine," she said at last. "You've got a deal, but not today. Come back tomorrow."

As Charlotte led Eleanor out of the room, both women chuckling at the exchange, Jayde felt a wave of relief wash over her. She'd done it. The project was on.

Alone in the small room, Jayde's eyes wandered, taking in the faded photographs on the dresser, the well-worn books stacked on the nightstand, and the delicate lace doily draped over the back of a chair. Each item whispered of a life rich with experiences waiting to be uncovered.

A thrill of excitement coursed through her, and Jayde couldn't suppress the smile spreading across her face. As she left the room, her mind whirled with questions and possibilities. Tomorrow, she knew, would mark the beginning of an extraordinary journey.

CHAPTER 3

As dusk settled over the city, Jayde sprawled across her bed, her phone held aloft, as she video-called Hannah. Her eyes sparkled with excitement as she recounted the day's events.

"That elderly woman, Eleanor, finally agreed to talk with me about her life," Jayde gushed. "So, she'll be my new subject."

Hannah's pixelated face creased with curiosity. "Do you think her story will be as interesting as that duplicitous company head?"

Jayde snorted, rolling onto her side. "I'd rather talk to a grumpy old woman than a corporate nightmare any day. I don't care how interesting his life is."

Hannah giggled, her laughter crackling through the phone's speaker. "He was totally unreliable. At least you know this old woman has a set schedule."

"There's just something about her that's intriguing," Jayde mused, her free hand gesturing as she spoke. "The way she tells a story, how she pulls things from around her at the moment to piece together a memory."

"Maybe you can get some advice from her," Hannah suggested.

Jayde chuckled. "I don't think that old bat is the type."

A sudden knock at the door interrupted their conversation. Jayde's brow furrowed as she peered through the peephole. Her heart skipped a beat when she saw Cesaro standing outside, fidgeting nervously.

"Cesaro?" she breathed, her earlier excitement evaporating.

Hannah's voice sharpened with concern. "Maybe you shouldn't answer it."

But Jayde's hand was already on the doorknob; her mind clouded with a mix of curiosity and residual affection. "I gotta let you go," she said absently, ending the call before Hannah could protest.

With a deep breath, Jayde opened the door, her face a mask of indifference. "What do you want?"

Cesaro's eyes darted past her into the apartment. "You won't let me in?"

"No." Jayde's tone left no room for argument.

Cesaro sighed, running a hand through his hair. "Fine, I'll say it out here... I want you back. Even if you go off and we have to do long-distance, I'm okay with that. I just need you in my life."

Jayde felt her resolve waver, but then she remembered all the reasons she had ended things in the first place. "That's too bad," she said flatly, slamming the door in his face.

Cesaro's muffled voice came through the wood, accompanied by frantic knocking. "Jayde! Open the door. At least think about it!"

Jayde leaned against the door, her heart pounding as she turned the lock. She listened as Cesaro's footsteps eventually faded away, leaving her alone with her turbulent thoughts.

The next afternoon, Jayde found herself back at the park with Eleanor. The autumn air was crisp, leaves drifting lazily from the trees as they settled onto a bench. Jayde clutched a small black plastic bag, its contents rustling as she sat down.

"I grabbed a few snacks from a nearby bodega," she said, reaching into the bag.

Eleanor wrinkled her nose in annoyance. "Stop crinkling that bag. It's annoying. You're ruining my peace."

Jayde ignored the older woman's grumbling and pulled out a package of Choc-Nut. "Let me introduce you to some Filipino snacks—"

To her surprise, Eleanor's eyes lit up. "Oh! Choc-Nut! I love these." She snatched the treat with unexpected enthusiasm, suddenly looking years younger.

"I traveled a lot in my younger days," Eleanor explained, unwrapping the candy with practiced ease. "I even spent a few months in the Philippines."

Jayde's eyes widened. "Really? I would love to travel, but my fiancé—well, ex-fiancé—didn't want me to. He wanted me to stay home, get a job at a local paper or magazine, and be around to raise kids."

Eleanor's gaze sharpened. "Do you even want children?"

The question caught Jayde off guard. "I... I don't know. I already feel like I have them. I'm the one who raises my two younger siblings most of the time. My aunt and uncle are around, but..."

"I figured you had some family issues," Eleanor mused. "The way you chastised that poor girl the other day made me wonder."

Jayde flushed with embarrassment. "I didn't chastise her... but yeah, things are far from ideal at home. My aunt and uncle are doing their best, but they work late. Even before they stepped in, I shouldered most of the responsibilities."

Their conversation was interrupted by the arrival of a young couple lost in their own world of newfound love. They strolled past, only to settle on the grass nearby with their picnic basket. The young man lovingly caressed the young woman's face as he gently pushed aside a lock of hair from her cheek. She fed him something from the basket, and they giggled, lost in their moment. He planted a kiss unexpectedly on her cheek; she reciprocated the gesture with an even longer one on his lips.

Eleanor sighed wistfully. "Oh, to be that young again."

Jayde rolled her eyes. "Oh, please..."

A mischievous glint sparked in Eleanor's eyes. "It's nauseatingly sweet, isn't it?" Despite her words, a hint of envy crept into her voice.

As they watched the couple's public display of affection, Jayde felt a pang of longing. "Why don't they just get a room and spare us?" she muttered under her breath.

Eleanor chuckled. "Come on, girl! The thrill of love or at least the initial stage of it. To be cradled in someone's arms, snuggling into his chest as if one is trying to merge souls. I do miss my time like that."

Jayde's cynicism softened. "I guess."

Eleanor leaned back on the bench, a faraway look in her eyes. "Here you go. Let me tell you about a time I felt like they do..."

Jayde quickly pulled out her small recorder. Eleanor's voice took on a dreamy quality as she began her tale, and Jayde found herself transported to another time and place...

Louisiana State University, decades ago. The library was a sanctum of hushed whispers and rustling pages. Eleanor, in her early twenties, sat at a table, her fashionable yet comfortable attire contrasting with the timeless tomes surrounding her. She was engrossed in a book about Ancient Egypt and Cleopatra, her brow furrowed in concentration.

The sudden thud of books hitting the table startled her. Eleanor looked up and locked eyes with a well-dressed young man who had unceremoniously dropped his belongings across from her. He wore confidence like a second skin.

She quickly averted her gaze, but he was not so easily deterred. He dragged his chair closer, eliciting death glares from nearby students. A flutter of nervous excitement stirred in Eleanor as she glanced up again.

"What are you reading?" he asked, his voice carrying a hint of genuine curiosity beneath his bravado.

Eleanor hesitated. "I'm working on a research paper about Cleopatra."

A grin spread across his face. "Now, that was a badass chick."

Rolling her eyes, Eleanor turned back to her book, but he leaned in closer, his dark eyes sparkling with intelligence and mischief. Against her better judgment, she felt drawn into his orbit.

"Come on," he coaxed, his voice low and persuasive. "You must have thoughts on Cleopatra's motivations."

The initial irritation faded as Eleanor met his intense gaze. "People say she was never satisfied—equating that with ambition—but I critique her for not being content with what she had."

He chimed in, "Because she had the love of two powerful men and bore their children out of that love."

Eleanor leaned forward, her eyes flashing with contention. "But did she truly love them? Did she even know what true love is? Or did she only see it as a seductress's tool for self-advancement and power?

Was she simply enacting her prowess at seduction, feigning loyalty as a political weapon?"

"Are you that jaded by love?" he challenged, a teasing smile tugging at the corners of his mouth.

Eleanor shook her head, a small smile playing on her lips. "No, what I am is a strong advocate of its idealism."

"Love cannot be charted in a straight line," he said, his gaze never wavering. "It's filled with tributaries and dams along its course."

"Ah, but you're talking about the journey," Eleanor countered. "The destination is clear, defined, and finite."

Their conversation flowed effortlessly from history to philosophy, the intellectual sparring igniting a spark Eleanor hadn't felt before. Despite her initial resistance, she had to admit—if only to herself—that this unexpected encounter was proving far more stimulating than any research paper.

Without warning, he leaned in close, his eyes like molten amber locked onto hers. "One day soon," he whispered, "I will kiss you."

Eleanor's breath caught in her throat, her heart a wild bird beating against her ribs. "You're... enigmatic," she managed, fumbling to gather her belongings.

His laughter, rich and warm, cascaded through the library, earning more disapproving glances that barely registered in Eleanor's whirling mind. "Don't be afraid," he murmured, his words like a soft caress. "My name is Emilio, and I've been inexplicably drawn to you every time I step into the library and see you sitting here."

"Should that not terrify me more?" Eleanor replied, her voice a mix of trepidation and undeniable curiosity.

As Emilio shared more of his story—a master's student who had been captivated by her presence—Eleanor's fear metamorphosed into *a flutter of anticipation. He was an enigma, and she yearned to understand him.*

In a bold moment that surprised even her, Eleanor heard herself ask, "Would you like to take a walk with me? By the river behind the university, perhaps?"

Emilio's smile bloomed like the first rays of dawn. "It would be my pleasure," he said, reaching for her bag. "Allow me."

With that small act of chivalry, Eleanor felt the last of her reservations crumble. As they left the library, a warm blush colored her cheeks, and she tucked a loose strand of hair behind her ear, her lips curving into a secret smile.

Their walk to the Mississippi River turned into a journey of discovery. When Emilio took Eleanor's hand, she didn't pull away; it felt like home. Under the sheltering branches of an ancient oak, with the river's steady song as their soundtrack, the world around them seemed to dissolve. The setting sun painted the sky in hues of gold and rose as if nature itself was blessing their encounter.

Emilio's arm around her felt both protective and adventurous. Their conversation flowed like the river beside them—sometimes slow and reflective, at other times a rush of confessions and shared dreams. Families, fears, ambitions—all laid bare as a bird serenaded them from above.

As twilight descended, Emilio turned to her, his gaze steady and filled with unspoken questions. Then, as softly as a whisper, inevitable as the river's flow, his lips found hers. The kiss tasted of promises and possibilities, of new beginnings and uncharted paths.

CHAPTER 4

The hum of the car's engine filled the silence between Jayde and Hannah as they drove through the city. Jayde gazed out the passenger window, her thoughts clearly elsewhere.

Hannah glanced at her friend, concern etched on her face. "Jayde, you haven't said much today. Are we... okay?"

Jayde blinked, pulled from her reverie. "Hm? Oh. We're okay, don't worry. I'm not thinking of anything bad. I'm just..."

"In a whimsical mood?" Hannah teased, a hint of amusement in her voice.

Jayde's lips curved into a small smile. "Eleanor told me an incredibly romantic story about a man she once met named Emilio."

As Jayde recounted Eleanor's tale of college debates and Mississippi River walks, Hannah found herself drawn in. "Wow! That really does sound like a dream," she exclaimed when Jayde finished. "Maybe she should be a writer too."

Jayde chuckled. "Well, that's why she's got me." A beat of silence passed before Jayde spoke again. "So, Cesaro came by again—"

"We're here!" Hannah interrupted, perhaps a bit too cheerfully, as she parallel-parked the car. "Come on! Wait until you meet this guy. He's really sweet and super talented!"

Jayde, momentarily stunned by the abrupt change of subject, exited the car and followed Hannah to a nearby building.

They climbed the stairs quickly, Hannah leading the way with an infectious enthusiasm that Jayde couldn't help but find endearing. At the top, they faced a large metal sliding door. Hannah pounded on it enthusiastically.

"Thani! It's Hannah!" she called out, her voice echoing in the hallway.

The door slid open with a soft whoosh, revealing Thani. He was a tall Peruvian man in his late twenties, his lanky frame draped in comfortable, bohemian clothing that made him look both casual and effortlessly stylish. His dark eyes widened slightly at the sight of Jayde, curiosity flickering across his face.

"You brought a friend?" he asked, his voice a pleasant baritone.

Hannah nodded vigorously. "Yeah! This is Jayde. She's my second set of eyes. I won't decide on anything without getting her opinion first."

Thani's eyebrows rose slightly, but he stepped aside with a gracious gesture. "If you say so," he replied, a hint of amusement in his tone.

As they entered Thani's loft, Jayde found herself lost in thought, her eyes roaming over the eclectic space. Art supplies were scattered about, half-finished canvases propped against walls, and the air smelled faintly of paint and incense. She was so absorbed in her observations that she barely noticed Thani's gaze lingering on her.

"Something on your mind, Jayde?" Thani asked, breaking through her reverie.

Startled, Jayde turned to face him, catching Hannah's encouraging smile as her friend made herself comfortable on Thani's worn but inviting couch.

"You can tell him!" Hannah urged. "It's a great story!"

Jayde hesitated, suddenly aware of the weight of both Thani and Hannah's attention. "Actually, I wasn't thinking of Eleanor this time," she admitted. "It's about Cesaro."

As Jayde narrated her recent encounter with her ex-fiancé, she noticed the shift in atmosphere. Hannah's fingers twisted nervously in her lap, her eyes darting between Jayde and Thani. Thani, for his part, leaned against his desk, arms crossed as he listened. His face remained neutral, but his eyes sparked with something akin to disapproval each time Cesaro's name was mentioned.

"He showed up at my apartment," Jayde explained, her voice tight with ambivalence. "He was all apologies and promises. He said he'd support my travel dreams this time and that he'd changed."

Thani let out a derisive snort. "Sounds like a real prince charming," he muttered. "What's next? He'll promise you the moon?"

Jayde felt a knot form in the pit of her stomach. The tension in the room was palpable—Hannah's nervous energy and Thani's barely concealed disdain for Cesaro created an uncomfortable cocktail of emotions.

Before the conversation could delve deeper into the complexities of Jayde's relationship drama, Thani turned to Hannah with a smirk, his voice a touch too dismissive. "Let's talk shop and forget about this guy, okay? Let me show you the book cover mock-up."

Grateful for the distraction, Thani moved to his desk and pulled out a 5"x 8" copy of a book. "Right, yes. Take a look at this," he said, holding it out to them.

Jayde leaned in, her breath catching as she took in the image. Two young women looked solemnly at the camera, their faces a study of conflicting emotions. Above them, in elegant script, was the title *Everlasting Ties by Hannah Jackson*.

Hannah, brimming with excitement, grabbed a pen from Thani's desk and scribbled a note inside the book, signing her name beneath it. With a flourish, she handed the book to Jayde, her grin infectious.

"To my first fan!" Hannah proclaimed with delight.

Jayde blushed as she closed the book, her fingers tracing the cover while Hannah's expression shifted slightly, hinting at disappointment.

The cover struck a deep chord in Jayde. It perfectly captured the complexity of female friendships—the bonds that could withstand trials and betrayals. She found herself reflecting on her own relationship with Hannah and the ups and downs they had weathered together.

Suddenly, Jayde placed the book in her purse and turned to Thani. "You did a beautiful job. The cover is really good."

"Thanks. I was trying to capture the sadness between the two friends while also conveying their hope," Thani explained.

"It really worked! Thanks again, Thani. We gotta go. We're already late," Hannah chimed in as she and Jayde made their way toward the door.

As they prepared to leave, Thani's parting words struck a chord in Jayde's mind. "We had to work today, but I'm a pretty good listener, and I'm almost always here," he said, his eyes meeting hers with an intensity that made her pulse quicken.

Jayde nodded, suddenly shy under his gaze. "Right," she murmured, following Hannah out the door. Just before it closed, she glanced back, catching Thani's warm smile and wave. It may not be the last time she found herself in this intriguing artist's loft.

Later that night, Jayde found herself at a nightclub with Hannah. The pulsing music mirrored the turmoil in her mind. They danced half-heartedly at the edge of the crowd, their focus more on their conversation than the beat.

"I really needed this to get my mind off things—off Cesaro, actually," Jayde admitted.

Hannah pulled her closer as a group of sleazy men eyed them. "Those guys are super creepy," she whispered in Jayde's ear.

They decided to head outside for some fresh air. The cool night breeze was a welcome relief after the stuffy club. Walking arm-in-arm down the sidewalk, they weaved through other partygoers. Jayde noticed Hannah stealing glances at her, a nervousness unusual for her.

Finally, Hannah took a deep breath. "I have to tell you something," she said, her voice trembling slightly. "I've got the courage to say this now, thanks to all the drinks. I know you don't want to talk about Cesaro, but..."

Jayde's stomach dropped, a sense of dread washing over her. "Don't ruin the night," she pleaded, though her words felt hollow.

Hannah stopped walking, gently unlinking their arms. She turned to face Jayde, her eyes glistening with unshed tears. "You can't go back to Cesaro. He's no good for you."

"You would know," Jayde snapped, bitterness seeping into her voice, surprising even herself.

Hannah flinched but pressed on. "I would know," she admitted. "That day you broke up with him... he came to my apartment. He told me you two had broken up for good a few days earlier, and I hadn't heard from you, so..."

The implication hung heavy between them. Jayde felt the ground shift beneath her. "Are you serious?" she whispered, her voice rising. "Did you sleep with him?"

Hannah's silence was all the answer she needed. "I... I don't know why I did it," she stammered. "But he lied to me, too. He said you two were done! For good."

Jayde's laugh sounded forced and bitter. "You could've asked me. But I guess you wouldn't, having wanted him back ever since the first time you slept with him. Hannah, it was a one-night stand sophomore year. You weren't even together."

"That's not true," Hannah protested weakly. "I don't want him. I don't even like him anymore. I don't know why I did it."

"Probably because you're selfish, insecure, and lonely." Jayde's words were hurtful, each one cutting deeper.

Hannah recoiled as if struck, her gaze dropping to the pavement. "Maybe you're right," she whispered.

A heavy silence fell between them, years of friendship unraveling in just a few devastating moments. Jayde's hand moved instinctively, pulling the book from her purse. "So much for sisterhood, huh?" she said, her voice cold.

With deliberate motion, she dropped the book into a murky puddle at their feet. The splash seemed deafening even in the noisy street. "You can live in your little fantasy world," Jayde said, her voice quivering with anger and hurt, "but in real life, actions have consequences."

Without waiting for a response, Jayde turned and stormed off, leaving Hannah standing alone on the sidewalk.

Hannah crouched down slowly, mechanically, as she retrieved the soaked book from the puddle. Water dripped from its pages as she shook it gently, her eyes fixed on the cover. With timid fingers, she opened it, revealing the words she had written earlier that day.

As she read the heartfelt dedication to friendship and loyalty, a sob rose in her throat. The irony was unbearable. What had once been a symbol of their bond was now a waterlogged reminder of how fragile it had always been.

Clutching the ruined book to her chest, Hannah wondered if, like the ink now running down its pages, their friendship had been irreparably smeared by the night's revelations.

CHAPTER 5

The sterile white walls of the Nerine Assisted Living facility's medical office seemed to close in on Eleanor as she sat upright on the examination table. Dr. Dorsey, a man in his sixties with kind eyes and a weathered face, perched on a rolling stool before her.

"I think we need to talk about a new plan for your health," Dr. Dorsey began, his voice gentle but firm. "Your disease isn't progressing quickly, but it is progressing."

Eleanor waved a dismissive hand. "It's fine, Doctor. I'm old enough already. I like my life and routine as they are."

Dr. Dorsey leaned forward, concern deepening the lines around his eyes. "Eleanor, I have to remind you that without intervention, every day could be a gamble. You're sure you don't want to consider treatment?"

"I'm sure!" Eleanor snapped, her patience wearing thin. "How many times are you going to ask?"

The doctor sighed, resignation settling over his features. "All right, all right. If that's how you feel, I can't force you. The best I can do now is to make you comfortable during the time you have left."

"That's what I want," Eleanor said firmly, sliding off the table. Dr. Dorsey stood to help her, but she waved him off, marching toward the door.

"Eleanor, if you change your mind..." His voice trailed off as she slammed the door behind her.

In the hallway, Eleanor strode purposefully, ignoring Dr. Dorsey's concerned gaze as he watched from the office doorway. She was so focused on her exit she nearly collided with Jayde, who had just rounded the corner.

"Eleanor!" Jayde called out, waving.

Eleanor clicked her tongue in annoyance and rolled her eyes, continuing past without breaking stride. Confused, Jayde glanced at the doctor before hurrying after the older woman.

"I know your hearing and vision aren't going, and I saw that eye roll," Jayde said, irritation creeping into her voice. "What's wrong?"

Eleanor remained stubbornly silent as they approached her room. Finally, she spoke, her tone clipped. "What are you even here for?"

Inside Eleanor's room, Charlotte was tidying up. She looked up as Eleanor entered, making a beeline for her dresser while Jayde settled onto the bed.

"Obviously, I'm here for the project," Jayde explained, "but now you've got me worried."

Eleanor huffed, pulling a cardigan from the dresser. "Stop fussing. You're so overbearing."

Charlotte, unable to contain herself, interjected, "Eleanor has been seeing Dr. Dorsey for some time—"

"It's just part of my routine," Eleanor cut her off sharply. "Have you forgotten about HIPAA?"

Charlotte's eyes flashed. "Have you forgotten why she's here?"

As Charlotte returned to her cleaning, an awkward tension filled the room. Sensing the need to break the silence, Jayde decided to share her own troubles.

"My best friend—well, perhaps she's not my best friend anymore. She's just... a former friend—"

"And what?" Eleanor interrupted. "Are you two fighting?"

Jayde nodded, her voice small. "Yeah."

"What about?"

"Hannah... she betrayed my trust."

Eleanor raised an eyebrow. "Sounds like you're not willing to tell the full story, either."

Before Jayde could respond, the sound of small feet and high-pitched giggles erupted from the hallway. Two young boys raced past the open door, narrowly avoiding impact with an exasperated orderly. Their mother hurried after them, her admonishments falling on deaf ears.

As the commotion faded, Eleanor's eyes took on a faraway look. "The joy and freedom of innocence," she mused.

"Hm?" Jayde prompted, curiosity piqued.

"All friendships are easy as long as there is innocence between the two people—when both are blissfully ignorant of selfish temptations," Eleanor explained. "Once that innocence is lost, that's when problems arise."

Jayde frowned. "I'm not sure what you mean."

Eleanor leaned back in her seat, her mind drifting to a long-ago memory. "I remember in my youth when I was seven, my best friend and I would play in the backyard. We climbed trees, complained about our parents and other friends, and planned what we would be doing later."

Eleanor's eyes glazed over, lost in recollection. Suddenly, Jayde could almost smell the fresh-cut grass and hear the laughter of children...

Young Eleanor, just nine years old, darted between the gnarled trunks of ancient fruit trees, her laughter ringing through the orchard. Hot on her heels was Cody, his clothes already smeared with dirt, a mischievous grin plastered across his face.

"You can't catch me!" Eleanor taunted, ducking behind a particularly large tree.

As she pressed her back against the rough bark, trying to stifle her giggles, a soft squeak from above caught her attention. Her eyes widened as she tilted her head back, gaze traveling up the trunk to a cluster of dark shapes nestled in the branches.

Before she could fully comprehend what she was seeing, Cody's hand slapped hard against her back. "Got ya!" he crowed triumphantly.

"Ow! Knock it off!" Eleanor yelped but quickly forgot her annoyance. "Look!" She pointed up at the tree.

Cody followed her gaze, his eyes lighting up as he spotted the nest of bats. For a moment, both children stood transfixed by the sight. Then, a familiar glint of mischief appeared in Cody's eyes—a look Eleanor knew too well, one that usually led to trouble.

"Let's see how high we can throw stones," he suggested, his voice low with excitement.

Eleanor watched, curiosity battling apprehension, as Cody scooped up a small pebble from the ground. With a swift flick, he launched it toward the nest. To their surprise, the stone hit its target on the first try.

Chaos erupted instantly. The bats, rudely awakened, burst from their roost in a flurry of leathery wings and startled squeaks. Eleanor and Cody threw themselves to the ground, screaming as the creatures swooped overhead.

As quickly as it began, the commotion subsided. The children cautiously lifted their heads, hearts still racing. That's when they saw it—one of the bats had fallen, its wing clearly injured by Cody's well-aimed stone.

Cody approached the creature first, his earlier bravado undiminished. Eleanor crept up behind him, torn between fear and concern for the injured bat.

With surprising care, Cody found two small sticks and used them to gently stretch the bat's wings. The creature lay still, its tiny chest heaving, dark eyes glinting with an almost otherworldly intelligence.

"It looks... magical," Eleanor whispered, leaning in for a closer look.

Before Cody could respond, a voice called from the direction of the house. "Eleanor! Cody! Where are you? It's time for lunch! Come wash up and eat!"

The spell broken, and Cody hastily dropped the sticks. The two children exchanged an awed glance before racing toward the house, the memory of the bat forever etched in their young minds.

"An hour later, we went back to the scene," Eleanor continued softly. "But the bat was gone. Had it returned to its nest? Strange, indeed! Still, what a find—and what a rush of adrenaline it gave us."

"You guys were little monsters," Jayde said, unable to hide her shock.

Eleanor chuckled. "Maybe so, but aren't all children a bit monstrous at some point?"

Jayde sighed, her shoulders slumping. "Especially as teenagers," she muttered under her breath.

Charlotte grumbled in agreement while Eleanor's gaze drifted to the window, her mind wandering through memories of her past.

"Cody and I always got into misadventures," Eleanor continued, her voice taking on a dreamy quality. "It could be as simple as a trip to the general store to buy bread for our families when disaster would strike..."

Young Eleanor and Cody ambled down a dirt road, the warm sun beating down on their backs. Eleanor clutched a basket filled with fresh bread while Cody swung a stick at the dilapidated fence posts they passed, punctuating the peaceful scene with the occasional 'thwack' of wood on wood.

Up ahead, a cow stood placidly by the roadside, tethered to a post and contentedly grazing. Cody's eyes lit up at the sight.

"Look! It's all by itself!" he exclaimed, excitement bubbling in his voice.

Eleanor rolled her eyes. "It's a cow, Cody. Who's going to mess with it?"

Cody's laughter should have been a warning, but Eleanor focused on their errand, continued down the road. It wasn't until she heard Cody's panicked shout that she realized something had gone terribly wrong.

"RUUUUNNN!!"

Eleanor spun around, her heart leaping into her throat as she saw Cody tearing past her, an enraged cow in hot pursuit. Without a second thought, she dropped the basket and fled, her feet pounding against the dusty road.

"You never beat me in a race!" Eleanor shouted, tears streaming down her face as she struggled to keep up. "How are you so fast?"

Cody, too focused on escape, didn't respond. The sound of the cow's hooves and the rattle of its dragging chain spurred them on, terror lending wings to their feet.

Just when Eleanor thought her lungs would burst, Cody's house came into view. Relief flooded through her—until Cody slammed the gate shut behind him, leaving her trapped on the wrong side.

"Cody!" Eleanor screamed, pounding on the gate as the cow bore down on her. "Let me in!"

Neighbors, drawn by the commotion, emerged from their homes. A brave man rushed into the road, brandishing a large broom at the advancing cow.

"Go on! Get! Get back!" he shouted, waving the broom threateningly.

The cow bellowed, more in surprise than anger, and turned away. As it lumbered back down the road, kicking up clouds of dust, Eleanor sagged against the gate, her heart still racing, while Cody erupted into hysterical laughter.

Jayde and Charlotte stared at Eleanor in horror.

"Mean little thing!" Charlotte exclaimed, shaking her head.

"You could've been killed!" Jayde added, her voice rising in disbelief.

Eleanor laughed, her tone rich with years of perspective. "Cody could be such an ass at times!"

"Why were you even still friends with him?" Jayde demanded. "He was awful!"

Eleanor's laughter softened into a wistful smile. "Maybe, but it's hard to let go of certain friends, especially when you've shared moments like that. Sure, it was Cody's fault, but we still experienced it together." She shrugged, her eyes twinkling with mischief. "Besides, it wasn't entirely one-sided."

A ghost of a smile played at the corners of Eleanor's mouth as her voice softened, recalling a long-ago summer day. "Once, he made slingshots for us and convinced me it would be safe to try them out in my backyard. He accidentally hit the window of a house two doors down, then grabbed both slingshots and ran straight home."

"The next day, when Cody came over, we watched seventy-six-year-old Mr. Reiner board up his window. Cody said he would go help him. I watched as he managed to get inside the property, and soon after, I saw Mr. Reiner angrily gesturing at Cody while he cried."

"To this day, I still feel terrible about being a silent co-conspirator," Eleanor admitted, her gaze distant.

When she finished, Jayde struggled to understand the point. "So, what's the takeaway here? He nearly let you get trampled by a cow, but it's okay because he didn't tattle about a broken window?"

Eleanor's expression turned serious. "First of all, I didn't break the window—I just happened to be there. I may feel guilty not standing with my friend, but I didn't do it. Second, there is no lesson. I'm not here to teach you about life. You're a grown woman—figure it out for yourself."

"Then why'd you tell me all that?" Jayde asked, clearly exasperated.

Eleanor raised an eyebrow, her expression incredulous. "Did you forget about that project? The one you begged me to help with. I'm the one who gets to choose the topics."

Realization hit Jayde. "Oh... right." She shook her head, feeling suddenly foolish. "I guess I was so wrapped up in what happened with Hannah that I—"

"If you want a lesson," Eleanor interrupted, her voice softening, "here's one: sometimes, everyone's an ass."

Right on cue, Jayde's phone rang. Hannah's name flashed across the screen. Jayde hesitated, Eleanor's words echoing in her mind. In that moment of indecision, she realized that the most important lessons weren't in grand revelations—they were found in the messy, complicated realities of relationships.

CHAPTER 6

The soft glow of dusk filtered through the windows of Thani's loft as he sat at his desk, fingers dancing across the screen of his art tablet. The rhythmic tapping of the stylus on glass was abruptly interrupted by a sudden, forceful knock at the door.

Startled, Thani rose from his chair and approached the door, sliding it open to reveal Jayde, her expression a whirlwind of emotions.

"Listen, I don't know why I'm here," Jayde blurted, her voice laced with frustration and confusion.

Thani blinked, taken aback. "...Okay," he managed, unsure how to respond.

Jayde shifted her weight, her eyes darting around the loft before settling back on Thani. "I just... wanted to talk to you. You said you're a good listener."

"I did," Thani acknowledged, his brow furrowing slightly. "Is Hannah with you?"

"No," Jayde spat, bitterness creeping into her tone. "She's probably prowling around for a taken man."

Before Thani could process her words, Jayde pushed past him into the loft. He closed the door behind her, his mind racing to catch up with the sudden turn of events.

"I guess I'll get you something to drink," he offered, grasping for normalcy. "What do you want? I've got—"

"Just water is fine," Jayde interrupted, sinking onto his couch. "It's gonna be a long night."

Thani raised an eyebrow, a hint of sarcasm creeping into his voice. "Oh, yeah? Not like I was busy or anything."

"Were you?" Jayde challenged, locking eyes with him.

Thani hesitated, then sighed as he moved to the kitchen to fetch a glass of water. As he filled it from the refrigerator filter, he stole glances at Jayde, who was now gazing out the window at the deepening twilight.

Returning to the living area, Thani handed her the water and settled onto the opposite end of the couch. They sat in silence for a moment, each studying the other.

"Are you going to tell me about Hannah or what?" Thani finally asked.

"No," Jayde replied flatly.

"Then what?"

Jayde took a deep breath. "How about my mom?"

"My mom… she's not a great mother. She never even wanted to be one, but she is. Three times over."

"You have siblings?" Thani asked.

"Yeah, I'm the oldest. Then there's Robin, and she's sixteen, and… well, you know what that's like. And Felipe—he's twelve, but he always looks like the weight of the world is on his shoulders."

"Sensitive kid?" Thani remarked.

"Yeah, he is. So, I've gotten stuck with—well, not stuck. I help raise them. I guess I could technically just run away at my age, but…"

"It's not something we want to do to our families. The kids didn't do anything wrong," Thani said softly, his voice understanding.

"Exactly. Did you have to look after siblings like that?" Jayde asked, glancing at him.

"No, they're out there, I'm sure. Somewhere. I grew up an only child, but my dad was... well, he had a lot of girlfriends."

"Oh. I'm sorry," Jayde said, her brow furrowing slightly.

"Meh," Thani shrugged. "It is what it is. My childhood wasn't tragic or anything. My mom was okay. Sorry about yours. What about your dad?"

Jayde hesitated, tracing the edge of her glass. "He left after Felipe was born. I'm surprised he held out that long, to be honest. My mom acts like an irresponsible teenager."

"Like your teenage sister?" Thani asked, half-smiling.

"Gosh, no. She's nothing like our mom. She's actually kind of responsible for her age. But she's still a kid."

"Well, she can still be a kid. From what I can see, she's in good hands. She's got you," Thani said gently.

Jayde took a slow sip of water, letting his words sink in. For a moment, she wasn't sure how to respond. Then something inside her loosened, and the floodgates opened. She began to talk—really talk—about her mother, Robin, and Felipe and the responsibilities she'd carried since she could remember.

Thani listened, his expression soft, offering small prompts and understanding nods. Their conversation flowed easily, with moments of shared understanding and even a few quiet laughs, the kind that comes from recognizing the same struggles in someone else's life.

"I don't know why I'm telling you all of this," Jayde admitted, cradling her now-empty glass.

Thani shrugged, a small smile playing on his lips. "Sometimes you just connect with somebody and trust them right away."

"Yeah, but why?" Jayde pressed.

"I'm not sure," Thani replied, leaning forward. "I just know it happens. I'm glad you find me comforting."

They exchanged smiles, a deepening of the connection drawing them closer until it was shattered by the sudden, jarring ring of Jayde's phone. She answered quickly, her face falling as she listened.

"Right... I'll go get them. Bye," she said, ending the call and standing up. "Thanks for listening. I have to leave. I need to pick up Tweedle-Dee from his friend's house and Tweedle-Dum from the movies."

Thani laughed as he took the glass from her. "How about I come with you?"

Jayde eyed him skeptically. "Why would you do that?"

"Why not?" Thani countered, a mischievous glint in his eye.

Jayde shook her head. Thani set the glass on the coffee table and blocked her path as she turned to leave.

"Don't you trust me?" he asked, a teasing tone in his voice.

"Shut up," Jayde said with a playful smile, rolling her eyes as she gently pushed him aside.

"Come on... I've got nothing else to do, remember?"

"I know you're lying, Thani."

"So what?" he retorted, grinning.

Jayde shook her head, exasperated. "Fine. Let's go," she finally relented.

Thani clapped, pleased with himself, and followed her out of the loft as they drove to pick up Jayde's siblings, the car filled with easy conversation and shared laughter. By the time they arrived at the Valencia home, Thani found himself deep in a discussion about movies with Felipe.

The house became mayhem. Robin complained about being ignored while Felipe and Thani excitedly chatted about art styles. Jayde tried to restore order, but the arrival of her uncle, Logan Valencia, Filipino, in his early fifties only added to the chaos.

Then the house phone rang, shattering the lively atmosphere. Felipe's face lit up as he answered, recognizing his mother's voice. But Thani noticed the room's mood shift dramatically. Jayde's expression hardened, her jaw clenched, and her posture tensed as she listened to the one-sided conversation.

"Mom! Where were you?" Felipe asked, his voice filled with concern and relief.

"I just got caught up at work, honey," Ilene's voice was smooth but tense. "Don't worry about it! Things will settle down soon, and everything will be normal again, right? This time, for sure."

"No more late nights and traveling? Are you sure?" Felipe's voice brimmed with hope.

"I promise, honey," Ilene replied firmly.

Before Felipe could respond, Jayde snatched the phone from his hand, her voice trembling with anger. "What the hell is wrong with you? How many times are you going to lie to him?"

Felipe looked at Jayde, eyes wide with confusion and hurt. Sensing his distress, Thani gently guided Felipe away, distracting him with talk of movies. "Tell me about that movie again. You can spoil it this time."

"But..." Felipe hesitated, glancing back at Jayde.

"Hey, I'll still watch it with you sometime," Thani assured him with a warm smile. "You can show me all the small stuff I'd miss without you."

Meanwhile, Jayde's heated words filled the background as she confronted her mother. "Don't call back here again! Robin and I don't trust you, but Felipe is still hanging on to your every word."

"Are you really going to talk to me like that?" Ilene's voice was incredulous.

"As long as you keep lying to Felipe—to all of us—I'll talk to you like this," Jayde snapped back.

"You can't talk to your mother this way," Ilene insisted.

Jayde's voice turned cold. "I wouldn't if I had one." She abruptly hung up the phone, tossing it onto the couch and burying her face in her hands.

Logan quietly approached, placing a comforting hand on Jayde's shoulder. "I think it's time for Felipe and Robin to get ready for bed."

Jayde looked up, nodding. "Yeah, of course. They've got school tomorrow. I've got to get Thani home, too."

After saying their goodbyes, Jayde and Thani left the house and drove back to his loft in near silence. Jayde sighed. "Sorry..."

"Hey, you warned me. Kind of," Thani replied, attempting to lighten the mood.

"That's why I had to pick them up. She just... 'forgot,'" Jayde muttered.

Thani nodded. "That explains what Felipe said."

Jayde hesitated before continuing. "I know we're supposed to respect our parents, but... I guess she's right. She is my mother."

Thani glanced at her. "I come from a culture like that, too, but tradition doesn't trump cruelty. Your mom is a toxic person, and you have no obligation to treat her like she isn't."

Jayde looked at him, surprised. "Your dad?"

"Eh. Both, honestly. I don't talk to either of them."

"You said your mom was okay."

Thani chuckled softly. "I lied. Didn't want to bore you with a sad story."

Jayde scoffed, then laughed. "Isn't it fun bonding over terrible parents?"

Thani smiled. "I'm sure lots of people do."

They pulled up in front of Thani's building, the hazard lights blinking rhythmically in the night. A moment of silence stretched between them.

"Thanks for being on my side," Jayde said softly.

"Anytime," Thani replied, more sincerely than he'd expected.

As Thani exited the car and walked toward his building, he glanced back to see Jayde's shy smile before she drove away.

CHAPTER 7

The soft morning light filtered through the window of Eleanor's room at Nerine Assisted Living, casting a warm glow on the elderly woman as she sat in her comfortable chair. Her keen eyes followed the movements of nurses, patients, and their families in the courtyard below, a silent observer of the facility's daily rhythms.

"Charlotte!" Eleanor called out, her voice tinged with irritation. "Have you gotten my medication yet?"

Charlotte emerged from the bathroom, drying her hands on a small towel. "You've already taken your morning medication today, Eleanor," she replied patiently.

Eleanor's brow furrowed. "Are you sure? My chest hurts. It always does when I miss it."

A flicker of worry crossed Charlotte's face. "You're having chest pains?" she asked. Without waiting for an answer, she strode to the wall-mounted patient call box and pressed the silent alarm.

"You don't have to do that!" Eleanor protested, waving her hand dismissively. "It's probably fine."

Charlotte stood her ground. "I'm your aide. We can't take any chances."

"There's no use bothering a doctor over it," Eleanor grumbled. "It doesn't even hurt that bad."

"I just told you," Charlotte said firmly, "we're not taking any chances."

Before Eleanor could argue further, Dr. Dorsey entered the room, a nurse close on his heels. The doctor's eyes swept the room, assessing the situation. "What's going on?"

Charlotte quickly filled him in. "She already took her morning medication at 8 a.m., as usual. It's about 9:30, but she says she's having chest pain."

Dr. Dorsey nodded, his expression solemn. "All right. Let me see what's going on here." He approached Eleanor as the nurse quietly closed the door behind them.

Eleanor huffed irritably as the doctor pressed his stethoscope to her chest, the cool metal contrasting with the warmth of the sunlight. The nurse efficiently took her blood pressure, the cuff tightening around Eleanor's arm.

After a moment, Dr. Dorsey straightened. "I think we should do some tests today," he said, his tone leaving little room for argument.

But Eleanor was having none of it. "Will you all forget about it?" she snapped. "I don't care. Let whatever it is happen."

Charlotte's voice was soft but insistent. "And what about everyone else?"

Eleanor's eyes flashed. "There's no one left to care."

A knock at the door interrupted the tense moment. Eleanor's exasperation was evident as she called out, "Now what?"

Jayde's head poked around the door, her expression morphing from confusion to concern as she took in the scene. "Crabby again? Oh—" She paused, acknowledging the presence of the doctor and nurse with a nod.

"Are you..." Jayde began, worry evident in her voice.

Eleanor cut her off. "Yeah, yeah. I'm coming. I'll meet you out front. Charlotte will help me."

Jayde's eyes narrowed suspiciously. "Okay..." She closed the door softly behind her.

As soon as Jayde's footsteps faded, Eleanor turned her glare on the medical professionals in the room. "Don't tell that girl anything," she ordered.

Dr. Dorsey protested, but Eleanor was already standing, her movements contradicting her earlier complaints of pain. "Forget those tests for today. I'm busy, as you can see."

"Eleanor—" Dr. Dorsey tried again.

"Just mark it down as AA or whatever it is. Against advice," Eleanor said dismissively.

"AMA," Charlotte corrected gently. "Against Medical Advice."

A ghost of a smile flashed across Eleanor's face. "There you go. You got it. Now, let's meet that girl."

With that, Eleanor strode out of the room, leaving the door open behind her. Charlotte followed, throwing an apologetic glance at Dr. Dorsey and the nurse, who was left to note the incident in Eleanor's file.

As Eleanor made her way to the front of the facility, her earlier pain seemed forgotten, replaced by a determination that Charlotte recognized all too well. Whatever was going on with Eleanor's health, it was clear she had no intention of letting it interfere with her plans for the day.

The park was quiet, save for the gentle patter of rain on leaves and the occasional distant rumble of traffic. Jayde and Eleanor sat side by side on a damp bench, huddled under the shelter of Jayde's umbrella. The cool mist in the air seemed to encourage confidence, prompting Jayde to open up about her recent frustrations.

"My mom claimed she couldn't pick up my younger siblings yesterday," Jayde began, her voice tight with suppressed anger. "She said she was 'caught up with work.' I ended up having to do it again."

Eleanor raised an eyebrow. "How do you know she wasn't?"

Jayde let out a bitter laugh. "She doesn't have that kind of job—if she even has one right now. That's usually what she says when she decides to go out partying, just to make it sound like she's being responsible."

Sighing, Jayde slumped her shoulders. "I know I had harsh words about that young mom before, but... at least she cried when her daughter was taken away. I think my mom went out and partied to celebrate."

Eleanor was quiet for a moment, her weathered face thoughtful. "Mm. She doesn't seem so bad now, does she? My mother wasn't all that great either. That's why I found that young one brave."

Curiosity piqued, Jayde turned to Eleanor. "What was your mother like?"

Eleanor's gaze grew distant as if she were looking into a past only she could see. "She was physically there but not emotionally or mentally. A teen mom—and not a nice one. It can be scary when teenage emotions take over. She liked to 'party,' too, bringing all kinds of men home."

"That sounds familiar," Jayde murmured.

Eleanor nodded, a sad smile playing on her lips. "You know, I found comfort in one of my schoolteachers. She was the closest thing I had to a mother figure. It felt like she was more like my real mother. I was always disappointed when it was time to go home."

As they continued to talk, their conversation wove through shared experiences of young, unprepared mothers and the impact it had on their lives. When Jayde asked if Eleanor's experiences had influenced her decision to abort years ago, Eleanor's response was immediate and firm.

"It certainly did. I wanted to break the cycle of neglect."

A thoughtful silence fell between them, broken only by the steady drip of rain from the umbrella's edge. Finally, Jayde voiced the question that had been nagging at her.

"Do you think your mother was brave? Like the girl from the park?"

Eleanor pondered this for a long moment, her eyes fixed on the misty park before them. "You know... I'm honestly not sure."

As the rain let up, Jayde found herself reflecting on the complexities of motherhood, family, and the choices that shape our lives. The park around them seemed to mirror her thoughts—a landscape of greys and greens, beautiful in its own way but tinged with a certain melancholy.

Later that evening, Jayde sat on the couch in the Valencia home, attempting to lose herself in a book while her siblings watched TV. The peaceful moment was shattered by a text message that brought a frown to her face. With barely concealed irritation, she rose to answer the door. When she opened it, Hannah stood awkwardly on the threshold, the tension between them apparent.

"I'm sorry for damaging your book," Jayde blurted out, her voice stiff and formal.

Hannah, taken aback, smiled softly. "It's all right. It actually made me realize there was more I wanted for the cover."

Jayde hesitated, unsure of how to proceed. "Why are you here?" she asked, turning back toward the living room.

Hannah followed her inside, her voice gentle. "About what you said before. You were right. I think we both need to think about getting back out there. There are other men besides Cesaro—for both of us. Separate men, of course."

Jayde chuckled but shook her head. "I'm not interested in another relationship right now."

"Who said anything about relationships?" Hannah replied, a teasing note in her voice.

Before Jayde could respond, the front door opened, and Ilene, a Filipina in her early forties, and Jayde's mother walked in. "Hello? I'm here!"

Felipe immediately rushed to her while Robin offered a reserved smile. Their excitement quickly faded when Ilene announced, "I'm just here for a brief visit."

Felipe's face fell, and Jayde, sensing the familiar pattern, stood up, anger simmering beneath the surface. "What?" she demanded.

Ilene waved her off casually. "I have to meet someone today. It came up last minute."

Jayde narrowed her eyes, suspicion creeping into her voice. "It's a man, isn't it?"

Ilene shrugged, defensiveness creeping into her tone. "Well, yes. Sometimes, people you have to meet are male."

"You know that's not what I meant," Jayde snapped, frustration boiling over.

Hannah, sensing the escalating tension, gently guided Robin and Felipe away. "Hey, guys, let's let them talk it out," she said softly.

Robin stormed off to her room, anger evident, while Felipe remained rooted to the spot, watching his mother and sister argue.

"Do you even care about them?" Jayde's voice quivered with emotion. "I know you never cared about me, but the least you can do is show Robin and Felipe some semblance of maternal regard. They're still kids."

Ilene sighed, her tone dismissive. "Oh, Jayde, you always act like this."

"Like what? An adult? One of us has to," Jayde retorted, her voice cracking.

Ilene glanced at her watch, clearly eager to leave. "I've got to go. I'll talk to you and your sisters again soon, baby," she said to Felipe, who didn't respond. He simply turned and retreated to his room, defeated.

As Ilene walked out the door, Jayde scoffed and turned to Hannah, bitterness laced in her words. "Don't you think my mother is having enough fun for both of us?"

Hannah's response was gentle and understanding. "I guess so. I'm sorry she's laying her responsibilities on you, Jayde."

Jayde's defenses finally collapsed, and the weight of her responsibilities crashed down on her. She sank onto the couch, tears spilling over. "Thanks for being here, Hannah," she said, her voice breaking.

Without a word, Hannah sat beside her, offering silent comfort. Jayde leaned into her, letting the sobs wrack her body, finding solace in the presence of a friend who empathized with her pain.

The following evening, Jayde found herself at Thani's loft, seeking a different kind of solace.

"It's open!" Thani called out, not expecting a visitor. When Jayde slid the door open and stepped inside, he looked up, surprised. His overalls were splattered with both dried and fresh paint from the canvas he was working on—a vibrant depiction of a sunny day in a field.

"Oh, hey, Jayde. Did Hannah send you? Is everything fine with the cover?"

Jayde shook her head, closing the door behind her. The loft, with its high ceilings and large windows, was bathed in natural light, casting a warm glow over the space. "She didn't send me. I just... I wanted to talk."

Thani wiped his hands on a rag, nodding thoughtfully. "And you thought of me again?"

Jayde hesitated, then sighed. "I don't really have anyone else to talk to."

"What about Hannah?" Thani asked, genuinely curious.

"She was with me last night," Jayde began, her voice tinged with lingering frustration. "Something my mom did. Hannah saw it, and she gets it... to a degree. But it's not the same as talking to someone who's been through the same thing."

Thani sighed, smiling sympathetically. "I get it. As long as you don't mind me working while we talk, feel free to share."

Jayde nodded, grateful for the invitation. She settled onto the couch, turning to face Thani as he resumed his work. The canvas before him slowly transformed under his skilled hands, each brushstroke adding life to the scene.

"Maybe it'll be therapeutic," Jayde contemplated with a weak smile. "Like art therapy."

Thani chuckled warmly, his laughter easing some of her tension. "Where do I start?" Jayde continued, more to herself than to him. "Well, I guess you already know about my relationship with my mom, so I'll just start with last night."

As she spoke, the words flowed more easily, spilling out as if they'd been trapped inside her for far too long. Thani listened quietly, occasionally nodding or offering soft comments, mostly allowing Jayde the space to express herself. The conversation ebbed and flowed like the strokes of Thani's brush, sometimes light and reflective, other times heavy with emotion.

Hours ticked by unnoticed. The sky outside the loft windows shifted from dusk to the inky black of night, and still, they talked. Jayde moved restlessly on the couch, her posture changing with her mood as she recounted the events of the previous evening—the confrontation with her mother, the bitter disappointment, the exhaustion of carrying so much responsibility on her shoulders.

A glint of light from a passing car streamed through Thani's loft window, momentarily blinding Jayde. She blinked, disoriented.

"It's morning already?" she asked, surprise evident in her voice.

Thani smiled, setting down his paintbrush. "Time always goes fast when you're talking about anything and everything."

Jayde nodded, a blush creeping up her cheeks as she realized how long she'd been there. "I really did, didn't I? I only meant to tell you about Mom, but then... I got into Eleanor and my ex."

"Conversations flow like that sometimes," Thani replied softly. "Especially if they're good ones with people you care to talk to."

Jayde's blush deepened as she grabbed her purse. "I guess that's true... Anyway, I'm sorry I took up so much of your time."

"It's all right. I didn't mind," Thani assured her.

"I'll see you later," Jayde said, moving toward the door.

Thani stood up from his stool, confusion visible on his face. "You're leaving? I'm not kicking you out."

"I know." Jayde smiled at him, a deep sense of gratitude welling up inside her. "Thank you. For listening. For... everything."

Thani returned the smile, setting down his brush. "Anytime, Jayde. You're always welcome here."

As she stepped out of the loft, Jayde felt as though she had discovered something precious in this unexpected friendship—a safe harbor in the storm of her life. She knew she had found someone who truly understood, and at the moment, that felt like the most precious gift of all. There was also a sense of lightness as if a burden had been lifted.

As the door closed behind her, Thani sank back onto his stool, a hint of melancholy crossing his face as he glanced at his painting. The canvas had transformed into a vibrant scene of a sunlit field, hope captured in oil paints—a stark contrast to the darkness they had shared through the night. While sunlight filled the space, it artfully illuminated a couch with a young woman sitting in a field of flowers, the woman bearing a striking resemblance to Jayde.

CHAPTER 8

Later that day, Jayde hurried toward the bench where she and Eleanor usually sat in the park. As she approached, she spotted Eleanor already there with Charlotte, irritation clear on the older woman's face.

"You're late!" Eleanor snapped as Jayde drew near.

Jayde paused and smiled. "I didn't realize you'd miss me so much."

"Why are you late?" Eleanor pressed.

Jayde sighed as she settled onto the bench next to Eleanor and Charlotte. "I got caught up in a class."

"Look," Eleanor said, pointing skyward. Both the sun and the moon hovered in the sky, a remarkable and beautiful sight.

"This is that time in the evening when you can see both the sun and the moon," Eleanor explained, her irritation forgotten in the face of the natural wonder. "Sometimes there's even a star next to its lunar sister."

As Jayde and Charlotte followed Eleanor's gaze, the older woman continued, "I wonder how many people take the time to marvel at God's evening magnificence in the sky. I always try to."

Charlotte seized the moment, handing Eleanor a small travel case of medication along with apple juice and cookies. As Eleanor took her pills, two men jogged past, their bodies glistening with sweat.

"I truly admire people who run for fun and health," Eleanor mused. "The dedication, stamina, and perseverance it requires."

Charlotte chuckled. "Right. I'm sure that's what we're all thinking right now."

As they giggled together, Jayde felt herself opening up. "Hannah says I need to 'loosen up.' Like, date, but... not necessarily a relationship, if you know what I mean."

Charlotte's eyebrows shot up. "Oh, the type of thing you don't really need a relationship for?"

As they laughed, Eleanor's eyes took on a faraway look. "Ha! Not me, that's for sure. Well, there was that one time in my youth!"

"Miss Eleanor!" Charlotte exclaimed, shocked.

Jayde leaned in, intrigued. "You've done that before? Just gone for something... physical?"

Eleanor's smile was enigmatic. "In a way, I suppose it was. But it wasn't just physical, not always. Amun was a hell of an experience."

"Amun?" Jayde and Charlotte echoed in unison.

Eleanor's voice took on a dreamy quality as she began her tale. "Oh, Amun... He was the co-owner of a boutique hotel in Giza, overlooking the pyramids. When our eyes first locked, it felt like we were two old souls reconnecting once again..."

The sun dipped below the horizon, casting a warm, golden glow over the pyramids. Eleanor stood by the window of her hotel room in Giza, her heart fluttering as she took in the view. The ancient structures, bathed in the soft light of dusk, felt like silent sentinels guarding secrets from millennia past.

A familiar voice broke her reverie. "It's beautiful, isn't it?" Amun's tone was soft, almost reverent.

Eleanor turned to see him standing in the doorway, his eyes reflecting the amber light of the setting sun. "It is," she agreed, her voice barely above a whisper. "I don't think I'll ever tire of this view."

Amun smiled and stepped closer. "Come," he said, offering his arm. "I want to show you something even more spectacular."

Curiosity piqued, Eleanor slipped her arm through his, and together they walked through the hotel, the warmth of his presence a comforting support beside her. As they ascended to the rooftop, the air grew cooler, and the first stars twinkled in the sky. When they reached the top, Eleanor gasped. The pyramids in open view were illuminated, glowing with an ethereal light that seemed to make them come alive.

"Wow," she breathed, unable to tear her eyes away.

Amun's gaze was fixed on her. "I knew you'd love it," he said softly.

They stood in silence for a long moment; the only sounds were the gentle breeze and their quiet breathing. Finally, Amun spoke again, his voice low and intimate. "You know, Eleanor, from the moment you arrived, I felt like I've known you forever."

She turned to him, her heart skipping a beat at the intensity in his eyes. "I feel the same way," she admitted. "It's like we're old souls reconnecting."

Amun's hand found hers, his thumb brushing lightly over her knuckles. "There's something special about this place," he murmured. "About us."

Their connection deepened over the following days. Even when Eleanor flew to Luxor, the bond between them remained unbroken. Each morning, his voice over the phone was the first she heard, filling the quiet of her hotel room with warmth. Each night, his words caressed her before she drifted off to sleep, a soothing balm against the loneliness of travel.

When she returned to Giza, Amun was there to greet her, and they picked up right where they left off. One night, he invited her on a Nile River cruise. Eleanor had never seen him look so dashing—his usual relaxed demeanor replaced by an elegance that took her breath away.

"You clean up nicely," she teased as they boarded the ship.

Amun chuckled, adjusting his tie. "I could say the same about you. You look stunning, Eleanor."

They spent the evening dining under the stars, the river shimmering beneath them like liquid silver. Conversation flowed easily, punctuated by laughter and quiet moments of shared understanding. By the time they returned to the hotel, the night had taken on a dreamlike quality, fueled by wine and the heady atmosphere of the rooftop party they attended after the cruise.

"Shall we dance?" Amun asked, offering his hand as soft music played in the background.

Eleanor smiled, accepting his invitation. They danced until the other guests retired, leaving them alone under the canopy of stars. The night air was cool against their skin, the scent of jasmine lingering on the breeze.

When they finally made their way back to Eleanor's room, she felt anticipation building between them. Amun's arm was steady as she leaned on him, her shoes dangling from her hand. When they reached her door, Eleanor fumbled with the key, laughing softly as Amun caught her arm to steady her.

"Here, let me help," he offered, his voice tinged with amusement.

"Thanks," she said, smiling up at him as the door swung open.

Inside, the room was dimly lit, the only light coming from the glow of the pyramids outside the window. As Eleanor sat on the edge of the bed, Amun remained standing, his gaze never leaving hers. There was a magnetic pull that neither of them could resist any longer.

"Tonight feels different," Eleanor whispered, her voice thick with emotion.

Amun nodded, his expression serious. "It does."

He took a step closer, then another, until he stood directly in front of her. Slowly, almost hesitantly, he leaned down and captured her lips in a kiss. It began gently but quickly deepened as the dam of restraint finally broke. Eleanor responded with equal fervor, her hands sliding up his chest, feeling the warmth of his skin beneath the fabric of his shirt.

The kiss grew more urgent, their bodies pressing closer, each touch igniting a fire that had been smoldering for days. Amun's hands roamed over her, tracing the curves of her body with a reverence that made her shiver. When they finally broke apart, both breathless, their eyes locked in a gaze of a loving, uninhibited release.

"Eleanor," Amun murmured, his voice husky with desire, "I've wanted this... you... since the moment we met."

She smiled, her heart pounding in her chest. "I know. So have I."

They kissed again, this time with even more intensity, losing themselves in each other. The world outside ceased to exist as they surrendered to the passion that had built between them. At that moment, they were not just two people—they were one, their bodies moving in perfect harmony, their breaths mingling, their souls intertwined.

As they lay together, spent and content, the cool desert air drifted through the open window, carrying with it the mystique of the pyramids. The ancient monuments stood silent and majestic, bathed in the glow of the night, witnessing the fervent passion that had exploded between them.

And in the quiet of the early morning, as Eleanor drifted off to sleep in Amun's arms, she knew she would carry this memory with her forever—a night when time stood still, and she was enraptured by the alchemy of the pyramids.

"Seriously," Jayde said, her expression a mix of incredulity and amusement as she shook her head. "When you put it like that, I wish I could have a night like that."

Eleanor leaned back, a satisfied smile on her lips as she shrugged casually. "With the right company, you can."

Jayde nodded, her expression thoughtful. "That's true… I guess there's no better time than now. I won't be around for the next couple of weeks anyway—spring break."

Charlotte's eyes sparkled with excitement as she leaned in closer. "Now that's the perfect time to start! Where are you thinking of going?"

Jayde hesitated, uncertainty crossing her face. "I'm not sure yet. I haven't really decided."

Eleanor's eyes twinkled with mischief, a playful grin spreading across her face. "I suggest Egypt."

The three women burst into laughter, the idea taking root in their imaginations. Jayde felt a spark of excitement ignite within her, the possibilities swirling in her mind. Maybe it really was time to create some stories of her own, stories she could look back on with the same fondness and awe that filled Eleanor's voice.

The exotic beach pulsed with energy as the night wore on. Music throbbed through the air, mingling with the sounds of laughter and crashing waves. Jayde found herself swept up in the crowd of spring breakers, her body moving to the beat as Hannah danced beside her.

"Seems like you thought about getting back out there!" Hannah shouted over the music, a knowing grin on her face.

Jayde laughed, the alcohol warming her veins and lowering her inhibitions. "I did! You win. I'll go for it, but... I'm still not sure about a relationship."

Hannah's eyes sparkled with mischief. "Don't worry; I don't think anyone here is, either."

As they laughed together, Jayde felt a sudden urge to confess. "Actually, I was... kind of interested in Thani."

Hannah's delighted squeal was almost lost in the noise of the party. "But the last time I saw him," Jayde continued, "I ended up just talking about what happened with my mom the night you stayed over."

"Ugh, Jayde. That's so like you!" Hannah teased. "You should definitely try again."

Jayde sighed, her mind drifting back to Thani's loft. "Isn't it unethical or something if you're working with him?"

"No, why? You're not his client. Just go for it."

As Jayde mulled over Hannah's words, her gaze wandered across the crowded beach. Suddenly, her eyes locked with those of a stranger—a well-built, attractive man with shoulder-length blonde hair.

Time seemed to slow as they smiled at each other, a silent connection forming across the crowd. Without looking away, Jayde gently backhanded Hannah, who spun around to see what had caught her friend's attention.

A grin spread across Hannah's face. "You know what? Sometimes, you just have to go for the next best thing."

Before Jayde could protest, Hannah was pushing her through the crowd toward the handsome stranger and his friend. "This is my friend, Jayde," Hannah announced. "She's shy."

Jayde felt her cheeks burn with embarrassment, but the man's amused smile and unmistakable Irish accent put her at ease. "Hello, Jayde, who is shy," he said, his Irish lilt sending a pleasant shiver down her spine. "I'm Ewan. I'm NOT."

"I'm not really that shy," Jayde countered, surprising herself with her boldness.

Ewan's eyes twinkled. "That's good!"

As Hannah and Ewan's friend drifted away into the crowd, Jayde found herself alone with this intriguing stranger. The music and the crowd seemed to fade into the background as Ewan leaned in closer.

"I've heard the beach is empty just a little bit away," he said. "It's probably easier to talk there."

Jayde felt a thrill of excitement course through her. "Let's go!" she said, grabbing Ewan's arm and leading him away from the crowd.

They walked along the shoreline, the sound of breaking waves a soothing counterpoint to the distant thrum of the party. The cool water lapped at their feet as they talked, getting to know each other under the vast, star-studded sky.

"How much longer will you be here?" Jayde asked, acutely aware of how little time remained of her spring break.

"A few more days. What about you?"

"I'm the same," Jayde replied. "There's a lot I want to see, but it would be a shame to go alone."

As they continued to chat, Jayde found herself drawn to Ewan's easy charm and adventurous spirit. The alcohol in her system made her feel warm and daring, and Eleanor's story of Amun replayed in her mind.

Looking out over the water, Jayde mused, "I wonder if this is what it was like to walk along the Nile."

Ewan's eyebrows rose. "The Nile? In Egypt?"

"It's just a story someone told me," Jayde explained, her thoughts drifting to Eleanor and her passionate tale.

"What's the story?" Ewan asked, interest evident in his voice.

Jayde paused, looking up at Ewan thoughtfully. She could feel her heart racing, the thrill of the unknown coursing through her. At that moment, she made a decision. "You know... I'm in school for journalism," she began.

"Okay," Ewan replied, clearly unsure where this was going.

"No, what I mean is... I'm always working on other people's stories—retelling theirs." She took a deep breath, gathering her courage. "I just want to make my own story for once."

With that, she stepped closer to Ewan, feeling the heat radiating from his body as she kissed him passionately. He was surprised at first but quickly complied, his arms wrapping around her waist and drawing her in as the waves crashed rhythmically behind them.

As they broke apart, both slightly breathless, Ewan grinned. "I'd be happy to be a supporting character," he said softly.

Their lips met again, the kiss mirroring the passion of Eleanor and Amun's encounter so many years ago. As the waves lapped at their feet and the stars twinkled overhead, Jayde felt as though she was finally writing her own story—one that was entirely hers.

CHAPTER 9

The baggage claim area buzzed with the usual airport chaos—tired travelers, squeaking luggage wheels, and the rhythmic clunk of suitcases tumbling onto the carousel. Hannah stood alone, absently scrolling through her phone, her own bag already at her feet.

Suddenly, a pair of hands grabbed her from behind. Hannah let out a startled yelp, spinning around to find Jayde grinning at her, eyes sparkling with mischief.

"Oh, my God, you scared me!" Hannah exclaimed, her shock quickly dissipating into amusement. "I guess you had a good time?"

Jayde's laugh was infectious, a melody of joy that echoed through the airport baggage claim. "You will never believe the last few days I've had," she said, her voice brimming with excitement. "Have I got a story for you?"

As Hannah hefted her luggage and Jayde retrieved her own from the carousel, the two friends fell into step, their closeness evident in the way they leaned toward each other, their voices low and conspiratorial as they navigated the crowded terminal.

Meanwhile, across town at Nerine Assisted Living, a very different scene unfolded. Eleanor perched on the edge of an examination table, her usual sharp wit dulled by the gravity of Dr. Dorsey's expression. The doctor sat before her on a rolling stool, a stack of papers in his hands that seemed to weigh more than they should.

Charlotte, Eleanor's aide, sat in the corner, a look of worry on her face, her fingers nervously tapping against her thigh.

"Eleanor," Dr. Dorsey began, his voice gentle but firm, "your results are not improving, nor are they even stabilizing. They've started to worsen, and the decline in your health is more than I'd like to see."

Eleanor's response was characteristically blunt. "So what?"

Dr. Dorsey leaned forward, his eyes meeting Eleanor's with an intensity that softened the clinical atmosphere. "Eleanor, I'm trying to tell you that you may not have much time left. Your heart is getting weaker every day."

A heavy silence fell over the room, broken only by Eleanor's dismissive snort. "And? I don't fear dying. I told you this before."

Charlotte's voice was hesitant when she finally spoke. "Perhaps you should tell Jayde. You've been spending a lot of time with her."

Eleanor's reaction was swift and fierce. "No! And you better not, either. I don't care how close you think you are to me; you're still my aide. And you're bound by HIPAA, right? So you can't. I'll sue you."

"Eleanor—" Charlotte began but was cut off by a sharp "Zip it!" from the older woman.

Eleanor slid off the exam table, her movements confusing her age as she stormed out of the room. In the hallway, she paused, one hand pressed to her chest, her breath coming in short gasps. Charlotte reached out to steady her, but Eleanor swatted her hand away, shuffling off down the corridor.

As Eleanor grappled with her mortality across town, Jayde was immersed in a different kind of struggle. She sat at an outdoor café, the sun casting warm rays across her table, a half-eaten croissant sandwich forgotten beside her as she focused on her phone, fingers flying over the keys as she texted Thani.

Their conversation flowed back and forth, a dance of ideas and gentle teasing.

"Is the news really worth it if all it does is tell us about the little annoying details of a celebrity's life?" Thani quipped.

Jayde's response was quick, her fingers barely keeping up with her racing thoughts. "The news is so much more than that. That's just what's popular."

As their exchange continued, touching on the value of journalism and the importance of shared experiences, Jayde found herself drawn deeper into the conversation. There was something about Thani that challenged her and made her think in ways she hadn't before. Her heart raced as she considered the connection they were building, each message a stepping stone across a vast emotional chasm.

Then, unexpectedly, Thani's tone in text shifted. "Contemplate a night out to dinner with me. Friday, at seven."

Jayde's heart skipped a beat. A thrill ran through her, but as she started to type a response—asking about the nature of their relationship—she hesitated, biting her lip and deleting the message before it was sent. What would she say? She sighed, setting her phone down and gazing out at the bustling street, her mind awhirl.

As if summoned by her thoughts, a taxi pulled up nearby. To Jayde's surprise, Ewan stepped out, his eyes lighting up as he spotted her.

"Jayde!" he called out, jogging toward her.

Jayde stood, confusion on her face as Ewan approached. They shared a brief, slightly awkward hug.

"Ewan! What are you doing here?" Jayde asked, still taken aback by his sudden appearance.

Ewan's smile was warm, a beacon of familiarity for her previous skeptical thoughts. "Internship program. I promise I'm not stalking you. My cab was driving past, and I looked in this direction... I didn't even know you were here."

As they fell into conversation, Jayde found herself torn. Part of her was drawn to Ewan's easy charm and the memories of their time together on the beach. But another part of her couldn't help but think of Thani—their deep conversations, the way he made her feel seen and understood.

When Ewan asked her to show him around, Jayde hesitated, her eyes darting to her phone on the table. After a moment's deliberation, she nodded, slipping her phone into her purse, the unspoken words between her and Thani still lingering in her mind.

As they set off to explore the city, Jayde couldn't shake the feeling that she was at a crossroads. The easy camaraderie she'd shared with Ewan on the beach seemed harder to recapture here, in her everyday world. Their interactions were cordial but distant, not like the intense connection she felt in her conversations with Thani.

Walking through familiar streets with Ewan, Jayde found her mind drifting. She couldn't help but wonder what path she was meant to take and who would be walking beside her when she did.

The soft glow of the bedside lamp cast long shadows across Eleanor's room as Jayde entered, her cheerful "Hey! Are you ready—" dying on her lips as she took in the sight before her. Eleanor lay on her bed, weak and exhausted, her usually sharp eyes dulled with fatigue.

"What's wrong? Are you alright?" Jayde asked, concern coloring her voice as she stepped closer, the warmth of her smile fading.

Eleanor's response was curt, lacking its usual bite. "Leave me alone. I'm just tired."

Jayde hesitated, torn between respect for Eleanor's wishes and her own worry. "Do you want to stay here today? I can just sit nearby—" She moved toward the chair by the window, but Eleanor cut her off.

"I said leave me alone!" Eleanor snapped, a flash of her old fire returning. "There is no story today! Why can't you just listen to me? Impudent little girl."

The words stung, and Jayde straightened, hurt and annoyance reflecting on her face. "Fine," she said, her voice tight as she moved toward the door. "I'm going to forgive you for today since it seems you're not feeling well."

Eleanor's retort was swift, with a bitter edge to her voice. "I don't need your forgiveness, nor have I asked for it!"

"Then maybe I won't!" Jayde shot back, adding in a quieter mumble, "I just wanted to see you again."

As the door closed behind Jayde, Eleanor's facade crumbled. "I didn't want to see you," she whispered to the empty room, her voice barely audible. "Not today..." With a shaky hand, she wiped away the tears that had gathered in the corners of her eyes, the weight of her isolation pressing heavily on her heart.

Later that night, Jayde sat at her desk, leaning back in her chair with a morose expression, the dim light from her lamp casting a glow over her scattered notes. Hannah lounged on Jayde's bed, her casual posture at odds with the tension that filled the air.

"So, how long has this been going on?" Hannah asked, propping herself up on her elbows. "A couple of weeks now, right?"

Jayde nodded, her eyes unfocused, staring into the distance. "Yeah. I've had a good time with Ewan, but it hasn't been the same as it was during spring break. It's different with Thani."

Hannah's eyebrows shot up. "Thani? You still see him?"

"We meet for lunch or just to talk, but nothing else has happened," Jayde explained, her voice trailing off as she recalled their deep conversations.

As their conversation unfolded, the complexities of Jayde's romantic entanglements spilled out in a torrent of confusion and frustration. She felt torn between Ewan's carefree charm and Thani's emotional depth, with the lingering shadow of Cesaro haunting her thoughts.

Hannah listened intently, offering advice and occasionally exasperated exclamations. "Will you worry about yourself for once?" she finally burst out. "We've got to get you sorted out. Now, what's going on with Thani?"

Jayde's response was hesitant, uncertainty creeping into her voice. "I don't know. We haven't exactly defined our relationship. Wouldn't he tell me if he didn't want me to speak to other people?"

As they dissected Jayde's feelings, comparing the physical connection with Ewan to the emotional bond she shared with Thani, Hannah's concern grew. "Are you thinking about a relationship again? I'm not sure that's a good idea so soon after Cesaro."

The mention of Cesaro opened another can of worms, and Jayde admitted he'd been asking to reconcile. Hannah's reaction was immediate and vehement. "Worst of all worlds! Listen...

Cesaro was awful to both of us, but to you especially. He's out of the picture. Write him off."

Their conversation was interrupted by a text from Thani, inviting Jayde out for a late-night snack. Her heart raced at the thought of seeing him again after having never agreed to his previous invitation to dinner. With Hannah's encouraging smile bolstering her confidence, Jayde decided to meet him, hoping to finally sort out her feelings.

Jayde and Thani ambled up the wide paths of the park, the evening air still warm from the day's sun. Around them, vendors packed away their wares from the vintage market, the day's bustle giving way to a quieter, more intimate atmosphere. They nibbled on Filipino snacks, the familiar flavors offering a comforting reminder of home.

As they approached the bench where Jayde often sat with Eleanor, she pointed it out, a wave of nostalgia washing over her. "That's where Eleanor and I always sit," she said, a hint of fondness in her voice.

Thani nodded, curiosity dancing in his eyes. "She's the person you've been interviewing, right?"

"Yeah," Jayde confirmed as they settled onto the bench, the wood still warm from the sun.

Suddenly, Jayde's phone pinged with a text. She glanced at it and then back at Thani, guilt tightening in her chest. "Oh, sorry. It's a text from..."

"Are you seeing someone?" Thani's voice was carefully neutral, but a flicker of hurt flashed in his eyes.

Jayde hesitated, her heart racing under the heat of his gaze. She swallowed hard, her voice barely above a whisper. "Well, sort of. Yes."

Thani's face fell, confusion and disappointment evident in his eyes. "I'm confused. I thought there was something between us, but... I guess not."

Jayde felt her heart constrict. "I... I'm not sure about what's between us," she admitted, her words hanging heavy in the air like a storm cloud ready to burst.

"You're not sure?" Thani's voice rose slightly, disbelief coloring his tone.

Jayde took a deep breath, bracing herself against the storm brewing between them. "Despite our connection, I've been thinking a lot about the future."

Thani's eyes flashed with hurt. "What's wrong with the future? Is it that bad if I'm in it?"

"Well..." Jayde hesitated, knowing her next words would wound him. "Your job isn't really stable, is it? Being an artist is tough, right?"

Thani's jaw clenched, hurt morphing into defensiveness. "It's not that tough. You've seen my place. You think it's cheap?"

"No," Jayde admitted, her throat tightening.

"It wasn't so bad that you couldn't pop over at night uninvited," Thani retorted, frustration simmering just below the surface.

Jayde felt her cheeks flush. "I did, but it's not like we were intimate."

Thani's sardonic laugh hovered in the evening air. "Is that what you need to be sure? I guess I should've been more aggressive in that aspect. I just thought what we had was beyond that."

The conversation spiraled rapidly, each word widening the gulf between them. Jayde's fears about financial stability clashed with Thani's hurt at her lack of faith in him. They touched on deeper issues—trust, commitment, and the nature of their undefined relationship—each revelation was like a fresh wound.

"Do you think being a reporter is easy?" Thani shot back when Jayde mentioned job instability. "There are probably plenty more people willing to do anything for a story. Better reporters than you."

"You don't have to get nasty," Jayde snapped, stung by his words.

"Why? Did you think about offending me?" Thani's voice turned cold; all pretense of neutrality was gone.

The air between them filled with tension. Finally, Thani stood, his posture rigid with hurt and irritation. "Forget it. We only need to be friends. All you had to tell me was that's what you're looking for."

"That's not what I said!" Jayde protested, frustration rising in her voice. "It's just that we never defined our relationship!"

Thani sighed, some of the fight leaving him. "That's true, but you could have asked. You didn't have to insult my job. I make more than you, though I personally don't find that important." He paused, his eyes meeting hers, searching for a flicker of understanding. "Let's define our relationship now so you're not confused. What do you want?"

Jayde hesitated, the intensity of the moment overwhelming her. In her silence, Thani found his answer. He nodded once, resignation settling over his features. "Okay," he said softly, then turned to walk away.

Panic flared in Jayde's chest. "Wait!" she called out, her voice cracking with desperation. "Can't I think about it?"

Thani didn't stop walking but called over his shoulder, his words carrying through the night air. "Sounds like you were doing a lot of that already. Goodbye, Jayde."

As Thani disappeared from sight, anger and frustration boiled over in Jayde. She kicked the bench hard, pain shooting through her foot—a fitting metaphor for the chaos of emotions she felt. Taking a deep breath, she tried to calm herself, but the turmoil inside her wouldn't subside.

Almost without thinking, she pulled out her phone and dialed Ewan's number. As the phone rang, guilt twisted in her stomach, but the anticipation of his voice was a welcome distraction. She needed to escape the mess she'd made with Thani, even if it meant complicating things further.

"Hello?" Ewan's voice came through, slightly groggy but warm.

"Sorry for disturbing you," Jayde said, her voice steadier than she felt. "I want to see you. Right now."

There was a pause, and then Ewan's voice, tinged with amusement, replied, "Is that so? Lucky for you, I'm not busy. Where do you want to meet?"

As Jayde arranged to meet Ewan, she couldn't shake the feeling that she was making another mistake. But the thought of being alone with her regrets was unbearable. She needed a distraction, even if it was one she might regret come morning.

The sky was just beginning to lighten with the first hints of dawn when Jayde found herself outside Hannah's apartment, knocking frantically. Her heart raced, overrun by the night's events that threatened to overwhelm her, leaving her breathless. Hannah opened the door, sleep still clouding her eyes.

"What happened?" Hannah asked, taking in Jayde's distraught appearance. "I thought you were with Thani?"

"I'm not," Jayde replied, her tone obscure.

Hannah's brow furrowed with concern. "Are you upset or relieved?"

"I don't know!" Jayde exclaimed, running a hand through her disheveled hair, her fingers trembling slightly.

"Okay, okay... Come in," Hannah said softly, stepping aside to let Jayde enter.

As Hannah closed the door behind them, Jayde launched into her explanation, the words tumbling out in a rush. "I tried to explain to Thani what I was feeling, but he stormed off. He said I insulted his job. I just told him I was worried about the future—the stability of a job as an artist."

Hannah stared at Jayde in disbelief. After a moment of stunned silence, she burst out, "Are you stupid?"

Jayde recoiled, shocked by her friend's bluntness. "What?"

"That wasn't even your problem in the first place!" Hannah exclaimed, throwing her hands up in exasperation.

"I know, I just..." Jayde stammered, collapsing onto Hannah's couch, the fabric cool against her skin. "As I was saying it, I realized that might be an issue too. Is there really any future if you're struggling financially?"

Hannah let out a groan of frustration. "Oh, my God. It's like you're sabotaging yourself. You know he makes more than you? And being a reporter isn't exactly stable, either. Anybody can spit out clickbait."

"That's exactly what he said," Jayde admitted, her voice small.

"Yeah, because it's true. It sucks, but it is," Hannah said, her tone softening as she sat down next to Jayde, placing a comforting hand on her back. "Besides, I never told you to PROPOSE to Thani. You're just supposed to start dating! How can you know any of those answers yet?"

Jayde was quiet for a moment, then let out a small laugh, the tension in her shoulders easing slightly. "Tonight... you and me. It really feels a lot like the old days. We don't feel so far away from each other anymore."

Hannah sighed, a mix of relief and regret in her voice. "I never wanted us to grow apart in the first place, Jayde. Cesaro just... got to me, I guess. I don't know. It was wrong, even if I thought he was telling the truth about you both breaking up."

"No, it's fine," Jayde said, surprising herself with the sincerity in her voice. "He was so good at it that it makes me wonder if it was even the only time. If you were the only one."

A heavy silence fell between them, their shared history with Cesaro hanging in the air.

"I AM sorry," Hannah said softly.

Jayde nodded, a small smile tugging at her lips. "I know. But... at least now I can see how awful he is. I don't feel so confused anymore."

"Awful, how?" Hannah asked a mischievous glint in her eye. "His personality or in bed?"

They both burst into laughter, the tension of the night finally breaking, the warmth of their friendship wrapping around them like a comforting blanket.

As their giggles subsided, Jayde grew serious again. "He's so selfish! I don't think he's ever even asked me how I felt."

Hannah nodded emphatically. "He doesn't! It's like you're barely even there. Other than that, though, in all seriousness—he is really manipulative. He made me feel like I was the only one for him, even though he had just left you."

"Cesaro has a way of tugging at the heartstrings of hopeless romantics. Or desperate ones," Jayde mused.

"What do you mean?" Hannah asked, her tone teasing. "Which one do you think I am?"

Jayde snorted. "I don't know. I think we're both."

As they continued to talk, dissecting their shared history with Cesaro and the complexities of their current situations, the mood lightened. Laughter replaced tears, and a sense of healing pervaded the room.

"Hey, let's do something really lame," Jayde suggested, her eyes sparkling with mischief. "Let's do a sleepover."

"Like teenagers?" Hannah asked, her eyebrows raised.

"Why not?"

Hannah hesitated, then reached for something on the coffee table. "I think you're forgetting something," she said, pulling out the battered, rain-stained copy of her book.

Jayde felt a surge of emotion as she took the book from Hannah's hands. "You grabbed it!" she exclaimed. "I didn't really mean to throw it away. I mean, I guess I did, but... I regretted it. I actually do admire what you've achieved."

They leaned back on the couch, their heads touching. "Can I get a reading from the author?" Jayde asked softly.

Hannah snatched the book playfully. "Fine!" She cleared her throat and read what she had initially written on the inside cover for Jayde: "No matter what obstacles you face, the best of friends will always find their way back to each other."

As Hannah's words hung in the air, both women felt tears prick at their eyes. They laughed at their own sentimentality, wiping away tears and basking in the warmth of their reconnection.

"Enough mushy crap!" Hannah declared, tossing the old book aside. "You have to hear the final edits. That one is old news." She grabbed a new copy of her book from the table, eager to share her latest work with her rekindled friend.

At that moment, curled up on Hannah's couch with the first light of day peeking through the windows, Jayde felt a sense of peace she hadn't experienced in a long time. Whatever challenges lay ahead—with Eleanor, with Thani, with her career—she knew she had a friend by her side. And for now, that was enough.

CHAPTER 10

The park was alive with the soft rustle of leaves and the distant chatter of passersby. Jayde and Eleanor sat side by side on their usual bench, sharing a Filipino snack—crispy lumpia and sweet, sticky turon—that had recently become a ritual of sorts during their meetings. The familiar flavors brought a sense of comfort, bridging their vastly different generations with every bite.

Jayde's eyes roamed the park, taking in the vibrant scenes of everyday life unfolding around them. Couples strolled hand in hand, their laughter mingling with the sounds of children playing nearby, while joggers pounded the paths, the rhythmic thump of their feet echoing in the background. Yet Eleanor seemed lost in her own world, her gaze unfocused and distant, as if she were watching a film that only she could see.

Two teenage girls walked by, arms linked and heads bent close in shared laughter. The sight stirred something in Jayde, reminding her of her own renewed friendship with Hannah.

"That reminds me," Jayde said, breaking the comfortable silence. "Things have been going really well with Hannah lately."

She reached for another piece of lumpia, noting that Eleanor had already finished hers, her hand hovering in anticipation for her to finish so she could reach in again.

"Is that so?" Eleanor murmured, her voice distracted and far away as if the words were drifting in one ear and out the other.

Undeterred by Eleanor's lack of enthusiasm, Jayde pressed on. "We even hung out overnight—a sleepover like when we were kids."

"Mmhmm..." Eleanor's response was noncommittal, her eyes still unfocused.

Jayde frowned, concern creeping into her voice. "Are you alright? You seem distracted today."

"I'm fine," Eleanor snapped, an icy edge creeping into her tone, causing Jayde to flinch.

"Come on, Eleanor. You can tell me what you're thinking about," Jayde coaxed gently, trying to bridge the gap that had suddenly widened between them.

Eleanor's eyes finally focused, sharp with sudden anger. "Why? Because that's our agreement? Because that's the only reason you see me?"

Jayde recoiled as if slapped. "What? That's not true. Of course, it was at first, but... today is such a nice day."

"Just forget about it. Leave me alone," Eleanor muttered, turning away, her frustration undeniable.

"Alright, I'm sorry," Jayde said softly, slouching slightly, hurt evident in the slump of her shoulders.

Eleanor sighed, her expression softening as she saw the effect her words had on the younger woman. "Don't mind me. I'm just a cranky old lady. It's not your fault."

A small smile tugged at Jayde's lips, the warmth of Eleanor's affection breaking through the tension. "I mean, you are a cranky old lady, but I'm happy we met. I'm glad you're warming up to me lately. This seems like it'll be a nice friendship for a long time."

Eleanor nodded solemnly, a shadow passing over her face. "Well... it will be for the rest of my life, anyway."

Jayde rolled her eyes, trying to lighten the suddenly morose mood. "Please. You're way too spry for that talk. Plus, you're stubborn. I know you too well for that to work on me now."

A ghost of a smile flickered across Eleanor's face, but before she could respond, they were both startled by the sharp honk of a car horn. A funeral procession rolled by, a long line of cars moving slowly down the street, somber and solemn. Eleanor watched it pass, and a deep sadness overcame her, the weight of memories hidden behind her gaze. Jayde, sensing a mood shift, turned her attention back to the park, giving Eleanor a moment of privacy with her thoughts.

The usual flow of stories and memories that marked their meetings was conspicuously absent. Instead, a heavy silence settled between them, filled with unspoken words and emotions neither was quite ready to voice. As the last car in the procession disappeared from view, Jayde found herself wondering what secrets Eleanor was keeping and what fears or regrets might be weighing on her mind. But for now, she simply sat in companionable silence, offering the quiet comfort of her presence as the world continued to move around them.

As they lingered in the silence, Jayde knew that there were no stories to be told today. But she also sensed that this stillness held its own kind of significance—a moment of connection amid the noise of life, a shared understanding that sometimes words weren't necessary.

The unexpected knock at her apartment door startled Jayde from her thoughts. She wasn't expecting anyone and a flicker of annoyance crossed her face as she opened the door to find Cesaro standing there, a hopeful smile on his face.

Before she could voice her irritation, Cesaro thrust two plane tickets into her line of sight. Jayde blinked, taken aback by the sudden gesture.

"What is that?" she asked, her voice a mixture of confusion and wariness.

Cesaro's smile widened. "I want you to know I'm serious about getting back together. We're going away for a while."

A laugh of disbelief escaped Jayde's lips. "Do I get a say? Or is this a kidnapping?"

"These go to England," Cesaro explained, ignoring her sarcasm, "but from there, we can go wherever you want."

Jayde was still confused. "Why England?"

"Haven't you always wanted to go there?"

"No," Jayde replied flatly. "Must have been one of your other girlfriends."

She started to shut the door, but Cesaro's scoff made her freeze, her eyes narrowing as she glared at him.

"What?" she snapped. "Did you honestly think this would win me back? That this would fix everything between us?"

Cesaro's confidence faltered for a moment. "I don't think it will, but it's a start. I'm willing to try. I know you want your freedom. I'll give it to you."

"How gracious of you!" Jayde's voice dripped with sarcasm, but a flicker of hope sparked within her—what if he really meant it this time?

Undeterred, Cesaro pressed on. "I'll support you when you need me. I'll pay for your plane tickets to follow whatever story your heart desires."

"Don't talk like a poet. It doesn't suit you," Jayde retorted. "Besides, I'm seeing someone."

A flicker of jealousy crossed Cesaro's face. "Does he have our history? Does he know you like I know you? Has he been there through your family troubles like I have? Does he even listen to you talk about your school articles?"

Jayde hesitated, her resolve wavering for a moment. "I... one of them does," she mumbled, the admission feeling like a betrayal.

"One of them?" Cesaro latched onto her slip, a glint of rage flashing in his eyes. Jayde remained silent, internally cursing her moment of weakness.

"I'll be exactly what you need," Cesaro continued, his voice softening. "You won't need more than one. You won't need anyone else but me. Neither will I! Just... think about it."

Before Jayde could respond, Cesaro leaned into her doorway and dropped the tickets on a nearby table. He turned and walked away, leaving Jayde standing in the doorway, her eyes fixed on the tickets.

"Just one..." she whispered to herself, her mind in a whirl. Should she go back to the familiarity of their past, or was she truly ready to embrace the unknown?

Before she could second-guess herself, Jayde found herself following Cesaro. She stood at the top of the stairs, and Cesaro stopped, looking up at her with hope and triumph in his eyes.

"One more chance," Jayde said, her voice barely above a whisper. "That's it."

A smile spread across Cesaro's face. "That's all I need. I'll make you proud."

He ascended the stairs, closing the distance between them in a few quick strides. Before Jayde could process what was happening, Cesaro's lips were on hers, kissing her with a passion that mirrored her encounters with Ewan. The naturalness of it sent a jolt through her system, memories of their past flooding back—the good and the bad.

As Cesaro led her back to her apartment, part of her screamed that this was a mistake, that she was backsliding into old patterns. But another part, the part that remembered the comfort of the familiar, allowed herself to be guided inside.

The door closed behind them with a soft click, sealing them off from the outside world. As Cesaro pulled her close once more, Jayde couldn't shake the nagging feeling that she had just made a decision that could change everything.

The aroma of sautéing garlic and onions filled Jayde's small apartment kitchen, the savory scent mingling with the tension in the air. But the sizzle of the pan was drowned out by Hannah's furious voice. Jayde stirred the ingredients mechanically, her shoulders tense as her best friend's words battered against her.

"Why would you ever go back to Cesaro?" Hannah demanded, her face flushed with anger. "You know how manipulative he is! What did he say to you?"

Jayde kept her eyes fixed on the pan, unable to meet Hannah's accusing gaze. "Nothing," she mumbled. "He just... Thani isn't answering my calls anymore, and Ewan is just a fling. He goes back to Ireland soon."

Hannah's laugh was sharp and disbelieving. "Are you insane? He wanted to keep you in a cage the last time you dated!"

"He swears he's going to try harder this time," Jayde protested weakly, but even she could hear the cracks in her voice. "Cesaro has never relented about me going on the road to work until now, and he even bought tickets this time. If he tries to trap me, then I'll just leave again."

"Well, leave now because he's already got you in a trap," Hannah retorted, her voice rising with frustration.

Jayde finally turned to face her friend, her own anger bubbling to the surface. "Hannah, Cesaro knows me like Thani does. Better, actually. And he can be as fun as Ewan... sometimes. It's like I said before—it's the best of both worlds."

Hannah's eyes widened in disbelief. "As fun as Ewan? Did you sleep with Cesaro again?"

The flush creeping up Jayde's neck was answer enough. "I mean... we are back together..."

"Jayde, he's nuts!" Hannah exploded, her voice filled with worry and exasperation. "Then he's been stalking and harassing me since you guys got back together. He tried to keep me, too. And when that didn't work, he devolved into a bully—just like he always does when he doesn't get his way. Look!"

Hannah thrust her phone into Jayde's face, and the screen was supposed to display a thread of increasingly disturbing messages from Cesaro. Jayde pushed the phone away, not wanting to see it.

"Dammit, Hannah!" Jayde snapped. "I thought you were over this obsession with Cesaro. But obviously not."

Hannah's face contorted with rage. "HE'S THE ONE WITH THE OBSESSION!" she screamed. "Why can't you see that?"

The tension in the room reached a breaking point. "Get out," Jayde said, her voice low and dangerous. She pushed Hannah toward the door—not roughly, but with enough force to make her point clear.

Hannah grabbed her purse, her hands shaking with anger. "You need to get out of this fantasy world you're living in," Jayde spat, her heart racing.

Hannah paused at the door, turning back to deliver one final blow. "You're the one living in a nightmare," she said, her voice tight with fury. "And you did it to yourself."

The door slammed behind Hannah with a finality that echoed through the apartment. Jayde stood frozen in the sudden silence, the smell of burning food finally registering. She turned off the stove mechanically, staring at the ruined dinner, her heart heavy with doubt.

As the adrenaline from the argument faded, uncertainty crept in. Had she made a terrible mistake? Was Hannah right? The questions swirled in her mind, but Jayde pushed them away, focusing instead on cleaning up the kitchen. She wasn't ready to face the implications of her decisions—not yet. For now, she would cling to the illusion of control, even as she felt it slipping away.

CHAPTER 11

The soft hum of medical equipment and muffled voices from the hallway filled the silence in Eleanor's room at Nerine Assisted Living. Eleanor sat motionless in her chair, her gaze fixed on a distant point beyond the window. The autumn leaves danced in the wind, their vibrant colors stark against the gray sky, but Eleanor barely noticed. Charlotte, her aide, watched her with concern etched deeply into her features.

"I have to stop seeing Jayde," Eleanor said suddenly, the finality of her words hanging heavily in the air.

Charlotte leaned forward, her brow raised. "I don't think that's wise. It's good for you to go out. You get fresh air, and you can reflect on your life with someone other than me or just by yourself. You don't want to lose all those stories, right? It's good for your memory to keep talking about them."

Eleanor's laugh was bitter, devoid of humor. "My memory isn't the problem, Charlotte. It's my heart! I won't even live long enough for my memory to fade."

Charlotte's voice softened. "You're already forgetful, you know. It's part of the—"

"I'm old," Eleanor snapped, cutting her off. Her eyes revealed a flicker of vulnerability. "Charlotte, I don't want that girl to watch me go like this. To deteriorate. To erode like a coastal cliff, losing pieces of myself to the tide."

Charlotte's gaze softened with understanding. "I know that you care about Jayde, and you're trying to protect her. But you have to let her decide what she wants, too."

Eleanor's gaze hardened a steely resolve beneath the softness of her age. "It's my life—my death. Don't forget that you're sworn to secrecy."

Charlotte sighed, a hint of sarcasm creeping into her voice. "Right. I don't want you to sue me."

Eleanor turned her head away, a frown deepening the lines on her face. Silence stretched between them, thick and uncomfortable. After a moment, Charlotte stood and quietly left the room, leaving Eleanor alone with her thoughts. As the door closed behind her, Eleanor's composure was dismantled; tears welled up in her eyes, spilling over as she confronted the reality of her decision.

Across town, the bustling college courtyard stood in contradiction to the quiet of Eleanor's room. Jayde emerged from one of the campus buildings, her mind preoccupied with thoughts of her upcoming meeting with Eleanor. The air buzzed with laughter and conversation, but she was lost in her own world. She barely noticed Cesaro until she nearly collided with him.

"Hey, babe!" Cesaro called out, a wide smile spreading across his face as he pocketed his phone.

Jayde blinked, momentarily thrown off balance. "Hey! I wasn't expecting to see you today. I mean, I'm glad you're here."

Cesaro's eyes sparkled with mischief. "I wanted to surprise you."

"I'm sorry, I don't have long today," Jayde said, already starting to move past him. "I have to go meet with Eleanor."

Before she could get far, Cesaro gently caught her arm, spinning her back toward him in a move that was clearly meant to be romantic. Jayde felt a flash of annoyance but couldn't help the small smile that tugged at her lips. She rolled her eyes, caught between irritation and amusement.

"Spend the day with me," Cesaro pleaded, his voice dropping to a conspiratorial whisper. "I have a whole romantic agenda planned out."

Jayde's resolve hardened. "I have to meet Eleanor. I'm nearly done with my project. I just need one more story from her."

As she turned to leave again, Cesaro's hand shot out, gripping her arm more firmly this time. "I'm ASKING you to stay with me," he said, his voice taking on an edge that made Jayde's skin crawl.

She frowned, taken aback by his sudden intensity. Seeing her reaction, Cesaro quickly released her, his demeanor softening. "I'm sorry, I just... I miss you. I want to make up for the time we lost and prove to you that I'll keep my word."

Jayde felt her anger dissipate slightly, but the unease remained. "Then keep it now," she said firmly. "I really need to see her. You promised to support me."

Cesaro took a step back, holding up his hands in surrender. "You're right, you're right. Have a good time."

As Jayde walked away, she couldn't shake the feeling that something was off. She glanced over her shoulder to see Cesaro's expression had hardened, a look of annoyance replacing his earlier charm. A shiver of worry ran down her spine, and she quickened her pace, suddenly eager to put as much distance between them as possible.

When Jayde finally arrived at Eleanor's room, the anxious energy from her encounter with Cesaro clung to her like a shadow. She barely had time to catch her breath before Eleanor's sharp voice cut through the air.

"Get out!"

Jayde blinked, taken aback by the vehemence in Eleanor's tone. "What? Knock it off, Eleanor. I've had a bad day already."

Eleanor's eyes flashed with irritation, her voice like steel. "Mine was fine. Until you showed up."

Jayde felt her patience wearing thin. "I'm serious. I'm not in the mood for this game. Can't we just drop this charade where you pretend to hate me?"

"Charade?" Eleanor echoed, her voice dangerously low.

Jayde's shoulders slumped, the fight draining out of her. "Please, Eleanor. I've already lost one friend this week; I don't feel like losing another."

A flicker of curiosity crossed Eleanor's face, her anger momentarily giving way to something softer. "Lost one?"

Jayde sighed, the words tumbling out in a rush. "Hannah and I had a falling out. Again. I don't know. I got back with my ex, and she went nuts."

Eleanor's eyebrow arched, her expression turning contemplative. "Is this the one who tries to trap you like a sickly baby bird?"

Despite herself, Jayde felt a small smile tugging at her lips. "Not you, too. But yes, it is. He isn't doing that this time, but... Hannah slept with him when he and I were broken up, and it was still fresh on my mind."

"So what's next?" Eleanor's bluntness was oddly comforting, a steadying force amid the chaos of Jayde's emotions.

Jayde hesitated, then the whole story came pouring out—Hannah's history with Cesaro, her suspicions about their continued involvement, her own confusion about whom to trust.

As Jayde's words trailed off, Eleanor growled low in her throat, pushing herself up from her seat with surprising vigor. "Follow me," she said begrudgingly, her tone brooking no argument.

Jayde found herself trailing after Eleanor. Whatever Eleanor had to show her, Jayde had a feeling it was going to be impactful.

The late afternoon sun cast long shadows across the manicured grounds of Nerine Assisted Living as Eleanor led Jayde into the yard. Small groups of elderly residents dotted the landscape, some wandering aimlessly, others seated on benches, their faces turned toward the fading warmth of the day. The air was fragrant with the scent of blooming flowers, and the distant sound of laughter floated on the breeze, momentarily lifting Jayde's spirits.

Jayde's eyes widened as she took in the scene. "This place is beautiful!" she exclaimed. "Why don't you sit out here more often?"

Eleanor's response was characteristically acerbic. "So I can avoid Chatty Kathys like you."

Jayde furrowed her brow in confusion. "What exactly am I supposed to be looking at?"

"This," Eleanor said, gesturing broadly. "Just this. These people are all living their lives, just like at the park. The park is just livelier."

As they stood there, Eleanor's gaze suddenly sharpened, focusing on something in the distance. "Watch THIS," she said, a hint of mischief dancing in her voice. Then, loudly, she called out, "Doris!"

Jayde followed Eleanor's gaze to see two elderly women walking arm in arm. One of them, presumably Doris, turned at the sound of her name. A small smile flickered across her face when she caught sight of Eleanor, but it quickly vanished when her companion shot her an angry glare.

Jayde couldn't help but laugh. "Snuffed by another grumpy old woman!"

"The grumpiest," Eleanor confirmed with a nod. "They are the Habershire sisters on their daily evening stroll. Lovely how close they have remained. But not to me."

"Have you known them a long time?" Jayde asked, her curiosity aroused.

Eleanor's expression softened due to creeping nostalgia and a hint of regret. "It's funny, or not funny at all, how once upon a time, the three of us were close."

"What happened?" Jayde asked, sensing a deeper story.

Eleanor sighed, her gaze drifting as memories flickered to life. "Friendships are complicated when men are thrown into the mix."

Jayde gasped, her mind jumping to conclusions. "Did she sleep with your man?"

"No, you idiot," Eleanor snapped, though there was no real venom in her words. Instead, a veil crossed her features. "Listen. We were best friends, but our friendship fell apart the night we were all gathered to celebrate Gladys' engagement to Dr. Brian Edmunds."

As Eleanor recounted the tale, the world around them seemed to fade away once again, replaced by the vivid memories of a night long past.

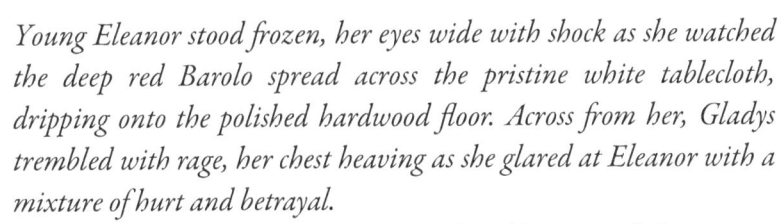

Young Eleanor stood frozen, her eyes wide with shock as she watched the deep red Barolo spread across the pristine white tablecloth, dripping onto the polished hardwood floor. Across from her, Gladys trembled with rage, her chest heaving as she glared at Eleanor with a mixture of hurt and betrayal.

"Damnit, Gladys!" *Eleanor finally found her voice.* "That was an expensive Barolo!"

Gladys's laugh was acerbic. "Fuck the wine!" *she spat.* "I see I have been your puppet for far too long; your kindness knows no bounds. Should I now marry your cast-off lover?"

Doris caught between her sister and friend, looked from one to the other in confusion and dismay.

"Good grief, Gladys!"

"Shut up, Doris," *Gladys snapped.* "I would hate to think you knew about this."

"I swear I did not!" *Doris protested, her voice high with panic.*

Why in the world would the idiot share with Gladys about my steering him in her direction and that we dated some years prior? As the argument escalated, the room seemed to spin around Eleanor. She tried to explain, her words tumbling out in a desperate attempt to salvage the situation.

"Gladys, listen to me," *Eleanor pleaded.* "Brian and I have always just been friends. We never slept together or even kissed. Back then, it was just one date."

"Who called it off?" *she asked.*

"It was mutual," *Eleanor answered, desperation creeping into her tone.*

"He said it was you!" *Gladys lashed out.*

How could a brilliant man be so stupid, especially on the night of his proposal? Or was it a confessional?

"So, let's see. Two years ago, you got me a job as his office assistant, and then you got me to be his fiancée, so now, do you have any tips on how long and hard I should ride him?"

"Gladys!" Doris screamed.

"Hey, you got yourself the ring; you must be doing it right," Eleanor responded, her heart racing.

"Ladies! Stop this at once!" Doris attempted to de-escalate the situation, her voice rising in urgency.

But Gladys was beyond reason, her pain and anger fueling a tirade that left no room for explanations or apologies. As accusations flew and tempers flared, Eleanor felt her well-intentioned meddling gone awry.

"Consider my strings cut," Gladys declared, her voice cold with finality.

In a dramatic gesture, Gladys yanked the engagement ring from her finger and tossed it across the counter. It skittered across the surface before disappearing amidst the shards of broken glass and pools of spilled wine.

Doris now acknowledged the mess and hastily attempted to clean it.

"Leave it," Eleanor murmured, her voice hollow with regret. "Spilled milk and all."

"Bitch!" Gladys stormed out, Doris trailing helplessly in her wake. Eleanor stood alone in the wreckage of the dining room; the ruins of their friendship reflected around her in the broken glass at her feet.

When Eleanor's story concluded, they found themselves back in the present, watching the Habershire sisters continue their stroll. Gladys pointedly ignored Eleanor while Doris kept sneaking glances back, regret in her eyes.

"Guess you never hashed it out," Jayde remarked, her tone laced with sympathy.

"How observant!" Eleanor's sarcasm was palpable, but her gaze remained fixed on the sisters.

Jayde pressed on, searching for meaning in the tale. "What's the lesson there?"

Eleanor's response was uncharacteristically cryptic. "You know what? For once, there is one: just let dead things lie. Let your friend go. Spilled milk and all. Or... should you?"

Jayde paused, confusion knitting her brow. "What? That's contradictory. Which is it?"

Eleanor didn't respond, instead turning to head back inside. Over her shoulder, she called out, "You tell me."

Left alone in the yard, Jayde reached into her bag and pulled out Hannah's damaged book. As she opened it to the first page and reread the opening line, a heavy sigh escaped her lips. Her mind spun with conflicting thoughts, Eleanor's story heavy on her heart.

CHAPTER 12

The streetlights flickered to life as Jayde and Cesaro emerged from the campus bar, their emotions heavy in the air.

"You don't spend any time with me!" Cesaro's voice was edged with frustration. "How can we repair our relationship if you focus on everything but me?"

Jayde's response was measured but firm. "This relationship needs to survive daily life as it is now before we can even think about hashing it out over the past."

Their argument was interrupted by a familiar voice. "Jayde?"

They turned to see Ewan approaching, his expression a mix of concern and hesitation. "Sorry to interrupt. I didn't hear much, but... are you all right?"

"Ewan? I'm fine—" Jayde began, but Ewan pressed on.

"I was trying to get a hold of you. Tonight is my last night in the city, and I was hoping to find you here."

Cesaro's face darkened. "Seriously? Do you not see she's with someone?"

"Doesn't really sound like she was having a pleasant time," Ewan countered, his gaze flicking between them.

As the tension mounted, Jayde felt trapped between the two men, her frustration growing. "Enough, both of you. Stop talking about me like I'm not here. Ewan, this is my... boyfriend. Ex-boyfriend. I don't know."

"You don't KNOW?" Cesaro and Ewan echoed in unison, disbelief flashing on their faces.

Before Jayde could respond, her phone rang. Seeing Robin's name on the screen, she answered quickly, her heart sinking at the panic in her sister's voice.

"I can't find Felipe!" Robin sobbed. "Mom was supposed to be watching him! I went to yell at him for borrowing my headphones, but he was gone! I can't find him anywhere!"

As Robin's frantic words poured out, Jayde felt her world narrow to a single point of focus. Her brother was missing. Nothing else mattered.

"Stay where you are. I'm coming to get you," Jayde said, her voice steady despite the fear gripping her heart.

Turning back to Ewan and Cesaro, she said simply, "I have to go."

Cesaro's reaction was immediate and selfish. "Right now? Are you serious?"

"My brother is missing!" Jayde snapped, her voice rising with anger. "Robin was out there looking for him!"

As Ewan voiced his support for Jayde leaving, Cesaro's true colors showed through. "No way, he'll find his way home. We're in the middle of something."

The argument that followed was ugly, with accusations of infidelity and questions of loyalty flying. When Cesaro called Jayde a "fickle, disloyal slut," it was Ewan who stepped in, placing himself between Jayde and Cesaro.

But Jayde didn't need protection. She pushed Ewan aside, her voice cold and fury. "Forget it! I don't have time for this! I'm going to look for my brother!"

As she stormed off to her car, ignoring Ewan's concerned protests, Jayde felt a strange mix of emotions: relief at escaping the toxic situation with Cesaro, worry for her missing brother, and underneath it all, a growing certainty that once again changes were on the horizon.

The car door slammed behind her, cutting off the sounds of the argument still raging as it spilled onto the sidewalk among onlookers. As Jayde pulled away from the curb, her mind raced ahead, focused solely on finding Felipe and bringing him home safely. Whatever consequences awaited her after this night, she would deal with them later.

For now, family came first.

Jayde's hands shook, her knuckles white as she gripped the steering wheel. She tossed her ringing phone onto the passenger seat, barely glancing at the screen. As she pulled away from the curb after dropping Robin off at the house, the device lit up once more, the words "NERINE ASSISTED LIVING" flashing across the display. Jayde shook her head, forcing herself to focus on the road ahead. Whatever it was, it would have to wait.

The city blurred around her as she drove, her mind racing faster than her car. Every red light felt endless; every turn was a gamble. She checked Felipe's usual haunts—the park, the library, his favorite comic bookstore—each empty space, another blow to her dwindling hope.

Finally, after reaching out to her aunt and uncle desperation led Jayde to the last place she wanted to be: the police station.

The fluorescent lights of the precinct were harsh after the dim streets, making her squint as she entered. The chaotic atmosphere amplified her rising panic, and her heart sank as she spotted Ewan and Cesaro sitting in the holding area. She shook her head in annoyance, deliberately ignoring them as she approached the desk clerk, her steps quick and purposeful.

"I need to report a missing child," she said, her voice tight with worry, hands gripping the edge of the desk.

The clerk's calm demeanor felt jarring in the face of Jayde's panic. "Was this recent?"

"Yes," she nodded frantically. "His name is Felipe Masipang-Rivera. He's—"

"Is that him?" the clerk interrupted, nodding toward an office behind her.

Jayde spun around so quickly that she nearly lost her balance. Her heart leaped into her throat as she saw Felipe sitting with a social worker. "Yes!" she cried, relief washing over her in a dizzying wave. She felt her knees go weak and had to grip the desk to steady herself.

As the clerk explained the situation—Felipe had come in claiming he was mugged, his phone stolen—Jayde barely listened. Her eyes were fixed on her little brother, drinking in the sight of him safe and sound. She noted his disheveled appearance and the tear stains on his cheeks, a mixture of relief and renewed worry flooding her.

When Felipe was finally brought to her, Jayde enveloped him in a fierce hug, feeling him trembling against her. She pressed her face into his hair, inhaling his familiar scent, reassuring herself that he was really there. The social worker's words about an impending investigation barely registered; all that mattered was that Felipe was safe in her arms.

"I'm so sorry," Felipe whispered, his voice muffled against her shirt.

"Shh, it's okay," Jayde soothed, running her hand over his back. "You're safe now. That's all that matters."

As they prepared to leave, Cesaro's voice cut through Jayde's relief like a knife. "Jayde!"

She turned, her patience finally snapping. Felipe tensed in her arms, and she instinctively tightened her hold on him. "Shut up, Cesaro," she hissed, her voice low but venomous. "In case you missed it, we are over. For good."

But even as she spoke, a nagging doubt gnawed at her. She remembered Hannah's confession, the hurt in her friend's eyes. "Have you been texting Hannah?" she asked, her voice low and dangerous.

Cesaro's denial was too quick, too vehement. "No! Why would I do that?"

With a sinking feeling, Jayde made a split-second decision. She turned to the desk clerk, her voice steady despite the turmoil inside her. "That man is my fiancé. Could I see his personal effects?"

The clerk, sensing the tension, handed over a bag of Cesaro's belongings without question. Jayde rifled through it, her hands shaking slightly as she pulled out his phone. She began scrolling through the messages, her face hardening with each swipe.

"Okay! Fine," Cesaro blurted, panic creeping into his voice. "We've been texting, but she started it. She can't leave me alone! I told her it was over—"

"That's not what any of this says," Jayde cut him off, her voice cold with fury.

"That... You don't know what you're reading. I'll explain it—" Cesaro stammered.

In a moment of pure catharsis, Jayde tossed the phone into a nearby trash can. The loud clatter it made as it hit the bottom was oddly satisfying. The clerk's amused smirk was the only acknowledgment of her small act of rebellion.

Turning to Ewan, who had remained a silent, supportive presence throughout, Jayde felt a surge of gratitude. "Ewan... I'll come back for you. Just let me get my brother home first."

Ewan nodded, his eyes warm with understanding. "Absolutely. I'm a big boy. I'll be fine." He turned to Felipe, his voice gentle. "Sounds like you had a rough day, buddy."

Felipe nodded silently, still clinging to Jayde.

As they walked toward the door, Cesaro's desperate voice rang out. "What about me?"

Felipe looked back, but Jayde gently placed her hands on his cheeks, guiding his gaze forward. "Don't look back," she whispered. "We're moving forward now."

With that, they exited the building, leaving Cesaro behind. The cool night air hit Jayde's face, and she felt as if she were stepping into a new chapter of her life. The road ahead was uncertain, but for the first time in a long while, she felt truly free.

The drive home was silent, the night's events hanging heavy in the air. Felipe huddled in the passenger seat, his eyes fixed on the passing streetlights, their glow casting fleeting shadows across his tear-stained face. Jayde's hands gripped the steering wheel tightly, her mind racing with worry and anger—a storm brewing inside her. As they pulled up to the house, she took a deep breath, bracing herself for the chaos she knew awaited them inside.

The scene that greeted them was worse than she had imagined. The living room was in disarray, and the furniture was askew as if a storm had blown through. In the center of the disarray lay their mother, Ilene, sprawled on the floor, drunk beyond reason. Robin, her face a mask of frustration and embarrassment, struggled to help her up. The sight ignited a fury in Jayde that had been simmering for years and about to boil over.

Without a word, she strode to the kitchen, her movements determined and purposeful. The sound of cold water rushing from the tap filled the tense silence; Felipe and Robin watched, wide-eyed, as Jayde marched back to where Ilene lay.

In one swift motion, Jayde upended a pot, dumping its contents unceremoniously over her mother's head. The shock of cold water cut through Ilene's drunken haze, her sputtering curses filling the air. But before she could fully react, Jayde's voice—low and deliberate, laden with years of pent-up frustration—cut through the room like a whip.

"I'm done," Jayde declared, her words resolute as a decree of judgment. "I've had enough. This was the last straw."

Ilene, water dripping from her hair and her makeup running in dark streaks down her face, struggled to sit up. "You little bitch!" she spat, her words slurred but venomous. "How dare you? I am your MOTHER!"

"As far as I'm concerned," Jayde retorted, her voice ice-cold, "none of us have one."

The dam broke. Years of resentment, disappointment, and pain poured out as Jayde and Ilene screamed at each other. Their voices rose and fell like waves in a storm, accusations and counteraccusations filling the air. Felipe cowered in a corner, hands over his ears, while Robin stood frozen, torn between intervening and fleeing.

The front door burst open, and Logan and Cassidy rushed in, alerted by the commotion. Logan moved to separate Jayde and Ilene while Cassidy gathered Robin and Felipe to try to shield them from the worst of the confrontation.

"Because of her neglect," Jayde shouted, her voice breaking, "Child Services are coming to investigate all of us now. They could take Felipe!"

At this, Felipe broke down, sobs wracking his small frame. "I'm sorry," he wailed, "this is all my fault!"

Jayde's anger softened for a moment as she turned to her little brother. "No, Felipe," she said gently, "this isn't your fault. It's hers." She pointed accusingly at Ilene, who now lay crumpled against the wall.

Logan took control and stepped between them. "Listen, all of you," he said, his voice firm but calm, "everything is going to be fine. This home is safe and comfortable."

Jayde laughed bitterly, gesturing wildly at the scene around them. "Is it? Look at her!" She pointed at Ilene, who was now slumped against the wall, her eyes unfocused and vacant. "Is she safe? Are WE safe?"

Logan's expression hardened. He turned to Ilene, his voice authoritative, leaving no room for argument. "I've done all I can for her as a brother. THIS FAMILY has done all it can for her, but she has to work things out on her own now. She won't be back. You hear me, Ilene?"

With Cassidy's help, Logan managed to get Ilene to her feet and escorted her toward the door. Ilene's protests and curses faded as the door closed behind them, leaving a ringing silence in their wake.

Jayde stood in the middle of the living room, her body trembling from the aftermath of adrenaline. Logan turned to her with concern. "You did the right thing," he began, but Jayde cut him off.

"Uncle Logan, please," she whispered, her voice hoarse from shouting, "I need a moment."

Logan nodded, understanding in his eyes. He squeezed her shoulder gently before leaving to join Cassidy and the kids upstairs.

Alone in the suddenly quiet room, Jayde felt the aftershocks of the night crashing down on her. With quavering hands, she pulled out her phone, desperately needing to hear a friendly voice. She dialed Hannah's number, only to be met with an automated message: "This number is out of service."

A strangled curse escaped her lips as she collapsed onto the couch. "What else could go wrong tonight?" she whispered to the empty room, her voice small and broken, echoing her feelings of helplessness.

As if in answer to her rhetorical question, her phone rang. Without looking at the caller ID—hoping against hope it might be Hannah—Jayde answered. "Hannah?"

"Hannah? No, it's me. Charlotte..." The aide's voice was hesitant and worried.

Jayde sat up abruptly, her heart racing. "Charlotte? Right! I forgot the nursing home called. What is it?"

The news hit her like a physical blow. Eleanor had been transferred to the hospital. Her heart nearly gave out. Jayde's mind reeled, trying to process this latest crisis.

"I'm coming right now," she said, already on her feet. "Which hospital?"

Charlotte's calm voice cut through Jayde's panic. "Calm down, hun. You both need to get some rest first. Visiting hours are tomorrow. Eleanor is fine; she's stable."

Despite Jayde's protests, Charlotte insisted. "She's all right. Just sleep and come up tomorrow. Visiting hours start at 10 a.m."

As the call ended, Jayde felt the last of her strength leave her. She curled into a fetal position on the couch, sobs wracking her body. The events of the night crashed over her in waves—Felipe's disappearance, the confrontation with Cesaro, her mother's drunken state, and now Eleanor's hospitalization. It was too much; all of it was too much.

In the quiet of the living room, with only the soft ticking of the clock for company, Jayde cried for everything she had lost and everything she feared she might yet lose. Tomorrow would bring new challenges and new decisions to make. But for now, she allowed herself this moment of vulnerability, this release of all the emotions she had been holding back for so long.

As the first light of dawn crept through the windows, Jayde's sobs finally subsided. Exhausted but somehow lighter, she drifted into a fitful sleep, her dreams a chaotic mix of hospitals, drunken mothers, and the steady, comforting presence of an old woman who had come to mean more to her than she ever could have imagined.

CHAPTER 13

The sterile white of the hospital room was softened by the gentle morning light filtering through the window. Jayde sat in an uncomfortable plastic chair beside Eleanor's bed, her body aching from the long night and the tension of recent events. Her gaze drifted between the peaceful face of her sleeping friend and the bustling world outside, where life continued its relentless march forward. The steady beep of monitors provided a rhythmic backdrop to her tumultuous thoughts—a reminder of Eleanor's fragility.

A slight movement from the bed caught Jayde's attention. Eleanor's eyes fluttered open, confusion quickly giving way to recognition and, surprisingly, annoyance. The older woman's face, lined with years of experience, contorted into a familiar scowl.

"Not you again," Eleanor grumbled, her voice groggy but sharp enough to cut through the hospital room's hushed atmosphere. "First, my heart gives out, and now you're here to chew me out."

Jayde leaned forward, guilt etched over her face. Recent events made her feel far older than her years. "I'm sorry," she said softly, the words barely audible over the constant hum of hospital equipment.

"Huh?" Eleanor's brow wrinkled, caught off guard by the apology. It wasn't often that Jayde showed such vulnerability.

"It's my fault. All of it," Jayde continued, her voice thick with emotion as she unleashed the words.

Eleanor struggled to sit up, her movements slow and painful. Jayde quickly moved to assist her, gently adjusting pillows and helping Eleanor find a comfortable position. "What the hell are you talking about, you brat?" Eleanor demanded, her tone softening slightly despite the harsh words. "You weren't even there."

As Jayde fussed with the bedding, she explained her fears, her voice trembling. "All the outings, demanding to talk to you... It stressed you out, didn't it? I pushed too hard, and now..."

Eleanor's laugh, surprisingly strong for someone who had just had a heart scare, cut through Jayde's self-recrimination. "Oh, please," she scoffed, rolling her eyes. "It was the same thing I did every day, anyway. You think a few conversations with you could take me down?" Her eyes narrowed suspiciously. "Charlotte called you, didn't she?"

"I plead the fifth," Jayde replied, a small smile tugging at her lips despite herself.

"Ha! I guess I'll let it slide," Eleanor conceded, settling back against her pillows. "Mostly because you look worse than I do. And that's saying something, considering I'm the one in the hospital bed."

Jayde's smile faded as quickly as it had appeared. "It was... a rough night," she admitted, her voice barely above a whisper.

Eleanor's expression softened almost imperceptibly. "Love me that much? Grow up," she scoffed, though there was a hint of warmth beneath her gruff exterior.

"No... Well, yes, but..." Jayde hesitated, then the words came tumbling out in a rush. She told Eleanor everything—about

WIND SHEAR: A NOVELLA 123

Cesaro's deceit, Ewan's unexpected appearance, and Felipe going missing as a result of her mother's drunken neglect.

Eleanor listened in silence, her expression shifting from surprise to concern to something akin to sympathy. When Jayde finished, Eleanor let out a low whistle. "Damn, all that in one night? You've been busy, kid."

Jayde nodded miserably, slumping in her chair. "To top it all off, Hannah's blocked me. I couldn't even talk to her about it. Not that I blame her. It was probably the worst day of my life—at least the worst in a long time."

"Well, unlike me, you've got plenty of time for an even worse one," Eleanor quipped, her dark humor shining through despite the circumstances.

Jayde's frown deepened. "Thanks," she muttered, but there was no real anger in her voice. She was too exhausted for that.

An awkward silence fell between them, broken only by the persistent beep of the heart monitor. The sound seemed to grow louder in the quiet, a constant reminder of Eleanor's mortality. Finally, Jayde spoke again, her voice barely above a whisper.

"I feel hopeless. I'm angry at myself for making stupid decisions that I knew were terrible. I'm angry at myself for not trusting my friend. I'm angry at Hannah for changing her number or blocking me. I'm angry at Thani for not responding to me. I'm angry at Ewan for... just existing, and I'm angry at Cesaro and Ilene because they're the most selfish people I've ever met."

As Jayde's litany of frustrations poured out, Eleanor's expression softened. When Jayde finally fell silent, Eleanor's response was unexpectedly gentle. "Everyone makes mistakes, kid. There was a time when I feared that every choice I made was a mistake. Every single one. Like now."

"Now?" Jayde asked, confusion evident in her voice.

Eleanor sighed, a flicker of vulnerability crossing her face. It was an expression Jayde had rarely seen on the older woman, and it made her heart wrench. "I'm sorry I didn't tell you sooner. Charlotte insisted that I should, but I didn't want you to see me like this. Weak. Vulnerable."

"It's okay. I understand," Jayde assured her, reaching for her bag. She pulled out a stack of neatly typed, stapled pages, offering them like a peace offering. "Do you want to see where all of your stories ended up?"

Eleanor's eyes lit up with curiosity, a spark of her old self shining through. "I can see it from here... But let me take a closer look."

As Eleanor flipped through the pages, a comfortable silence fell over the room. The only sounds were the rustling of paper and the beeping of machines. Eleanor's fingers traced the words on the page, a small smile playing at the corners of her mouth. At that moment, the hospital room faded away, and they were transported back to the park bench where their unlikely friendship had begun.

"We worked on a lot of memories, didn't we?" Eleanor mused, her voice filled with nostalgia.

Jayde nodded, then asked hesitantly, "Did you ever feel hopeless?"

Eleanor's gaze grew distant, lost in memories. "I'd broken up with the love of my life to gain freedom, but it all went downhill from there."

As Eleanor recounted her struggles—working on her doctorate, haunted by past decisions, missing the lover she'd left behind—Jayde found herself drawn into the story. She saw parallels with her own life that she'd never noticed before, a shared experience of love, loss, and the struggle to find oneself.

"How did you get through it all?" Jayde asked, leaning forward intently.

Eleanor shrugged a gesture that seemed to encompass a lifetime of resilience. "I just did."

"Why didn't you just go back to what you knew?"

Eleanor's response was firm, her eyes meeting Jayde's with an intensity that belied her frail appearance. "You need to be brave if you want to move forward."

"Fortune favors the bold," Jayde quoted, a hint of her old confidence creeping back into her voice.

"Bah!" Eleanor waved her off, her familiar gruffness returning. "That's not always true. Look at us."

Jayde flipped through the pages again, and her brow furrowed in thought. Suddenly, she sat up straight, her eyes wide with realization. "You're right. That last quote... doesn't work for us. But you know what does? 'Freedom lies in being bold.'"

Eleanor's smile was warm and genuine, pride shining in her eyes. "Robert Frost," she acknowledged with approval. "You're learning, kid."

They shared a moment of understanding, their shared stories and hard-won wisdom passing between them in a single look. Then Eleanor clicked her tongue, waving Jayde away with a familiar gesture. "Get out of here. Go be bold."

As Jayde stood to leave, she paused in the doorway, suddenly reluctant to go. "I'd like to turn this into a book," she said hesitantly, "but I... I just don't like the ending we have."

Eleanor's eyes twinkled with mischief, a hint of her old spirit shining through. "FINE. I'll need to think about it. Get out of here."

"You keep that copy. I have others," Jayde said, knocking on the wall—a gesture that had become their own private ritual.

As the door closed behind Jayde, Eleanor sighed, looking down at the papers in her hand. A smile played at her lips as she read, losing herself once more in the memories they had shared. At that moment, despite the hospital setting and the uncertainty of her health, Eleanor felt a sense of peace. She had lived a life worth telling, and in Jayde, she had found someone to carry those stories forward.

The holding cells at the city jail stood at odds with the vibrant world outside. Ewan and Cesaro were confined to separate cells, each contemplating their predicament in unique ways. Ewan lounged on the narrow bed, a relaxed posture unbothered by his situation. In contrast, Cesaro paced restlessly, his movements erratic, like a caged animal yearning for freedom.

The echo of footsteps down the corridor captured their attention. A jail officer appeared, and to their surprise, Jayde accompanied him.

"Ewan Byrne!" the officer called out. "You made bail."

Ewan looked up, confusion washing over his face. When his gaze landed on Jayde, a smile broke across his features. "Well, look who it is!"

Cesaro's reaction was immediate and desperate. He lunged for the bars of his cell, gripping them tightly. "Jayde!" he called out, his voice a mixture of hope and urgency. "Let's go home."

Jayde's response was cold and decisive. She clicked her tongue, refusing to meet Cesaro's gaze. "I'm not here for you," she said flatly. "You can rot." Turning to Ewan, her tone softened just slightly. "Let's go."

As Ewan exited his cell, he couldn't resist giving Cesaro a small wave. The gesture pushed Cesaro over the edge. "Jayde!" he shouted, his voice reverberating off the concrete walls. "You fucking cunt!"

Ewan turned, muscles tensing for a confrontation, but Jayde pressed forward, guiding him away. The officer's hand hovered near his belt, ready for trouble, but Ewan allowed Jayde to lead him outside.

The bright sunlight was almost painful after the dimness of the jail. Ewan squinted, adjusting the bag of personal effects in his hand. "Thanks for not leaving me in there," he said, genuine gratitude coloring his tone.

Jayde shrugged, her expression unreadable. "It never crossed my mind."

"Really?" Ewan asked, surprised. "Why not?"

Her answer was simple and honest. "Cesaro is clearly an ass while you stuck up for me." She paused, choosing her next words carefully. "But, Ewan... this needs to be goodbye."

Ewan nodded, understanding shining in his eyes. "Fair enough. Bit hard to come back from that, right?" A hint of his usual charm returned as he added, "Call me if you change your mind, though."

A small smile tugged at Jayde's lips. "I'll think about it," she said, her tone suggesting she wouldn't.

Just then, Jayde's phone rang. The screen displayed Charlotte's name, but when Jayde answered, Eleanor's voice greeted her.

"Oh, good, it does work," Eleanor said, her dry humor evident even over the phone. "It's me."

"Eleanor?" Jayde's surprise was palpable.

"Do I sound like Charlotte?" Eleanor retorted.

As Jayde explained the events at the jail, Ewan took his cue to leave. He waved goodbye, his departure marked by a surprising lack of drama. Jayde returned the wave absently, her focus already shifting back to Eleanor's questions.

In the days that followed, Jayde found herself swept up in a whirlwind of activity. She penned a final letter to Hannah, echoing the sentiment from Hannah's book about best friends always finding their way back to each other. The letter was taped to Hannah's door—a peace offering and a hope for reconciliation.

Thani proved more elusive. When Jayde knocked on his door, she was met with silence. Understanding the unspoken message, she left without protest, accepting that some bridges, once burned, couldn't be easily rebuilt.

Life continued its relentless march forward. Social workers inspected the Valencia home, and their approval felt like a weight lifted off Jayde's shoulders. In what felt like the blink of an eye, graduation day arrived. Donning her cap and gown, she accepted her diploma amidst the cheers of her makeshift family—Logan, Cassidy, Robin, Felipe, and, to her surprise and delight, Eleanor and Charlotte.

Weeks later, Jayde once again was seated beside Eleanor on their familiar park bench, the air charged with the promise of new beginnings.

"I'm finally going abroad," Jayde announced, unable to contain her excitement.

Eleanor's response held her characteristic dry humor. "You think that sleazy guy will be at the airport, trying to stop you?"

Jayde laughed, shaking her head. "Cesaro? God, I hope not."

As their laughter faded, a more somber mood settled over them. Jayde's thoughts turned to Thani, her voice wistful as she admitted, "Actually, I was really hoping to see Thani again, but..."

"You haven't spoken to him?" Eleanor asked gently, sensing Jayde's regret.

Jayde shook her head, struggling to find the right words.

Recognizing the need for a change of subject, Eleanor gestured to the manuscript in Jayde's bag. "Anyway, we still need a good ending for our book."

"YOUR book," Jayde corrected automatically.

"OUR book," Eleanor insisted. "You're writing it."

As they debated ownership of the story, Eleanor's eyes took on a faraway look. "Did you ever settle down?" Jayde asked, curious about that undisclosed part of her friend's life.

Eleanor nodded, a soft smile playing on her lips. "I did get married. To the love of my life."

"Who?" Jayde pressed, leaning in. "Emilio? Amun? It's not the father of the fetus, is it?"

Eleanor's eyes sparkled with memories of a distant past as she began her tale. Jayde leaned closer, captivated by the promise of the last chapter in her friend's extraordinary life.

"I had finally found my freedom," Eleanor said, her voice taking on a dreamy quality. "I successfully completed my doctorate and was heading to Florence. I had heard of an underground wine cellar that had been refurbished and converted into a restaurant..."

The cool, damp air of the wine cellar enveloped me as I descended the stairs, guided by a friendly maître d'. The soft glow of candlelight danced off the ancient stone walls, creating an atmosphere of intimate mystery. The scent of aged wood, rich wine, and savory dishes wafted through the air, tantalizing my senses.

"I love these hidden, hole-in-the-wall places," I murmured, my eyes drinking in every detail. The rough-hewn beams overhead, the worn yet polished wooden tables, and the mismatched vintage chairs—all spoke of history and authenticity.

The maître d' smiled knowingly, a twinkle in his eye. "You'll really love this place. I promise," he said, his Italian accent adding to the charm of the moment.

As we wound our way through the restaurant, I felt as if I were stepping back in time. The low murmur of conversations in various languages, the clink of glasses, and the occasional burst of laughter created a warm, inviting atmosphere. The rustic charm of this modest establishment was exactly to my taste.

The maître d' led me to a small table tucked into a cozy alcove. I settled into the seat, my fingers tracing the smooth, worn surface of the table. I ordered a top-shelf wine, savoring the ritual as the sommelier presented the bottle, and poured a small amount for taste. The rich, complex flavors of the Tuscan wine danced on my tongue.

For the meal, I chose a half Florentine steak with salad, which, I thought, any more was too much for one person.

The steak was perfectly cooked, the meat tender and flavorful, beautifully complemented by the crisp, fresh salad. Yet, as delicious as the food was, it was the ambiance that truly captivated me. As I savored the meal, my gaze roamed over the room.

The other diners formed a fascinating mix of locals and tourists. At one table, an elderly Italian couple shared a bottle of wine, their fingers intertwined on the table, speaking volumes about a lifetime of love. Nearby, a group of American tourists excitedly discussed their plans for the next day, their voices a bit too boisterous but brimming with enthusiasm. In a corner, a solitary businessman scribbled furiously in his planner, pausing occasionally to take in a mouthful of his pasta.

I felt a wave of contentment cover me. This was why I traveled—to experience moments like this, to feel connected to a place and its people, even if just for an evening.

Midway through my perusal of the room, my eyes locked onto a familiar face across the way. For a moment, time seemed to stand still. The candlelight flickered, casting shadows that danced across the silhouette's features, making it hard for me to be sure of what I was seeing. Yet there was something in the set of the shoulders, the tilt of the head, that sent a jolt of recognition through me.

My heart raced, a mix of excitement and apprehension flooding my senses. Could it really be him? Here, of all places? I blinked, half-expecting the illusion to vanish. But when I opened my eyes, he was still there, his gaze fixed intently on me.

At that moment, I felt as if all the noise in the restaurant had faded away, leaving only the sound of my own quickened heartbeat. I was acutely aware of every detail—the weight of the fork in my hand, the lingering taste of wine on my tongue, the rough texture of the stone wall against my back.

As the stranger rose from his seat, I experienced a strange mix of anticipation and fear.

"Who?" Jayde's excited interruption brought Eleanor back to the present. She smiled smugly, enjoying her listener's eagerness.

"This magnetic force emerged from his dinner party of fellows," Eleanor continued, her voice rich with memory. "He pulled a chair over to my solitary table, took the unused wine glass from the table across from me, and poured himself a glass of Chianti from my bottle."

The wine cellar restaurant hummed with soft conversation and the clinking of glasses, but for me, the world narrowed to the man standing here. My heart raced, its thunderous beat drowning out all other sounds. The years melted away in an instant, and I was once again the much younger woman who had fallen hopelessly in love with him.

"Emilio," I breathed, his name falling from my lips like a long-forgotten prayer—both familiar and strange on the tongue.

Emilio stood there, somehow both exactly as I remembered and entirely different. The years had been kind to him, adding distinguished lines around his eyes and a touch of silver at his temples. But his smile—that roguish grin—was the same one that had captured my heart all those years ago.

He lifted the glass of Chianti, his dark eyes never leaving mine. "I think I should have this first," he said, his voice a rich baritone that sent a shiver down my spine. It was exactly as I remembered, perhaps even more potent after years of absence.

With a fluid motion, he drank the entire glass in one go, his Adam's apple bobbing as he swallowed. I watched, transfixed, as he sat down and poured himself another. I sat quietly, my hands clasped tightly in my lap to hide their trembling, observing him with a mix of shock and growing warmth. The years seemed to dissolve, leaving only the intensity of our shared history to engulf us.

"How long are you here for?" Emilio asked, breaking the charged silence. His tone was casual, but there was an undercurrent of agitation.

"Five more days," I replied, surprised at how steady my voice sounded despite the turmoil inside.

Emilio nodded, a flicker of something—disappointment? Hope?—passing over his features. "How long has it been since we last saw each other?"

I hesitated; the weight of our separation suddenly heavy between us. "Emilio..." I began, unsure how to navigate this unexpected reunion.

"Almost fifteen years," he finished for me, his tone cool yet edged with annoyance. I winced.

As we caught up on the years that had passed, I felt a whirlwind of emotions threatening to overwhelm me. I spoke of completing my PhD, my voice gaining confidence as I discussed my academic achievements. Emilio, in turn, shared stories of his work with fellow anthropology professors, his hands animating his words in a way that felt achingly familiar.

"So, what do you think of Florence?" Emilio asked.

"I think it's beautiful and steeped in rich history."

He laughed. "Well, now that you've given your customer review for a tour, I'll ask again—what do you really think of Florence?"

When Emilio pressed me again, I couldn't help but launch into a passionate discourse on the city's colonialist view of Alessandro de Medici. As I spoke about the erasure of the first Black head of state in the modern Western world, I saw a familiar spark ignite in Emilio's eyes—the same look he had during our late-night debates in college when we discussed history and politics until dawn.

My words came faster, fueled by my passion for the subject and perhaps a desire to impress him. "Alessandro de Medici has been reduced to a footnote. Imagine a museum dedicated to the Medici family that doesn't even acknowledge his existence. The general community will only describe him as a tyrant who died by assassination, when in fact, he was the first Duke of Florence backed by

Pope Clement VII, a Medici himself, and Charles V, the Holy Roman Emperor, who also avenged his murder."

As I continued, delving into the complexities of Medici history and Florence's selective memory, Emilio leaned forward, his eyes shining with interest—and pride.

"As far as a tyrant, many of the Medici leaders before him were accused of being such, yet they are revered. Also, let us be honest: there is little in Florence that has not been impacted by the Medici, including their influence on the Renaissance. So why so little on Alessandro? Is it because of his African heritage? A question I would honestly like answered."

Emilio slapped the table excitedly, startling nearby diners. "That's my girl!" he exclaimed, his voice filled with admiration and nostalgia. My heart skipped a beat.

I blushed, the years falling away. At that moment, I was once again the young woman who had fallen deeply in love with this brilliant, enigmatic man. The intensity of my feelings, long thoughts buried by time and distance, rushed back with a force that left me breathless.

"Emilio," I said softly, my voice thick with emotion. "I'm sorry."

The words hung above us, heavy with the weight of our shared past—the love we had shared, the dreams we had, and the painful separation that had torn them apart. Emilio's smile faded, replaced by an unreadable expression that made my heart clench.

After a moment of tense silence that felt like an eternity, Emilio reached into his wallet and extracted two hundred euros, placing them deliberately on the table. The gesture was both generous and slightly aggressive—a clear statement that he was taking control of the situation.

"Let's go," he said, his voice leaving no room for argument. There was a glint in his eye I recognized—a mixture of determination and barely contained emotion that both thrilled and terrified me.

Emilio stood and extended his hand to me. I hesitated for a moment, but when he leaned in close and whispered in my ear, "Walk," I rose and followed his instruction. Though no longer the young, impulsive woman I had been when we first met, the pull I felt toward Emilio was as strong as ever.

With a deep breath, I placed my hand in his, feeling the familiar warmth and strength of his grip. As we walked out of the restaurant, I was silent, and my curiosity piqued about where he was leading me. Suddenly, I tripped, but he caught me, only to then burst into laughter.

"Are you still a klutz?"

"It's the unevenness of these cobblestone streets!" I protested.

"No, you've always had two left feet." I scowled at him, but at least his mood had shifted.

"Have you been to the Arno River?" he asked.

"Not at night, but I plan to sometime in the upcoming days."

"It's nearby; let's check it out."

We arrived at the Ponte Vecchio bridge, crossing over the Arno. The lights along the banks shimmered in the moonlight. Emilio released my hand.

"Why did you leave me?" he asked softly.

"Our paths were going in different directions. You were focused on your master's and then your doctorate, and I wanted to study abroad before graduation," I explained.

Emilio suddenly slammed his hands against the wall I had propped herself against. His arms stretched above either side of my head, his face inches away from me. With cold, glassy eyes staring into mine, he whispered sternly, "Ancillary truths—what's the real reason?"

My gaze darted away. Closing my eyes, a single tear streamed down my cheek as I blurted out, "I wanted to be free. Not from you—I loved you—but I needed to not feel shackled for a while. I needed to be free."

Emilio withdrew, restoring my personal space. I regained my composure, and we stood in silence, looking across the Arno.

After a long pause, he asked quietly, "Was I holding you back?"

"No, but over time, I would have felt like you did. Everything I did, I factored you in. I needed more time for personal growth."

He braced himself against the wall, running a hand through his hair. To my relief, I noticed no ring on his left hand.

"Are you with anyone?" I asked timidly.

He smirked. "No."

I rushed to embrace him, resting my head on his chest. "I'm so sorry. I did love you; I STILL love you!"

He sighed as if unspoken words had been finally released and returned my embrace. I have never forgotten how safe I felt in his arms. He lifted my chin to look into my eyes, asking if I was attached to anyone. I shook my head. Then, he kissed me ever so lightly.

"It's late. Let me walk you to your hotel. Where is it?" he asked.

"Just two minutes from the Duomo," I answered.

I felt frustrated and disappointed that after unleashing so much emotion, all that was left was for him to walk me back to my hotel.

We walked in silence for a few minutes, Emilio holding my hand, expertly guiding us through the maze of streets. Suddenly, I stopped and let go of his hand.

"I don't mean to upset you again," I began, "but is this it? Do you have nothing else to say? I say I—"

Emilio pulled me to him and kissed me with a voracious hunger that let loose my own. When he let go, he looked into my eyes and asked, "What are the odds we find each other again—in Florence, Italy? I'm taking you back to your hotel, but I have no intention of letting you out of my sight ever again. Is that all right with you?"

Blushing, I lowered my gaze and nodded. He took my hand again. "Now, walk faster," he said with a grin. I giggled and picked up the pace.

The cobblestone streets stretched before us, promising an adventure I hadn't anticipated when I set out for dinner that evening. Whatever lay ahead, I knew this unexpected reunion with Emilio would change the course of my life once again, leading me toward the love and freedom I'd always sought.

Epilogue

The sun-dappled park was alive with laughter and the distant hum of traffic. Golden leaves drifted lazily from the trees, forming a patchwork carpet on the ground. Jayde and Eleanor sat on their usual bench, a sense of contentment settling over them like a warm blanket.

Jayde leaned back, a smile playing on her lips, her eyes sparkling with admiration as she looked at Eleanor. "That's a perfect ending," she said, referring to the story Eleanor had just shared—a tale of love, loss, and rediscovery.

Eleanor's smile was wistful, her gaze distant. The lines on her face seemed to soften as she reminisced. "For a book, maybe," she replied, her voice carrying the experience of years. "For me, it was just a new beginning."

Jayde pondered these words, marveling at the wisdom they held. She had come to treasure these moments with Eleanor; each conversation felt like a gift, expanding her understanding of life's complexities.

As if on cue, Charlotte's car pulled up to the curb. The sleek sedan gleamed in the afternoon sun, augmenting the park's natural beauty. Charlotte stepped out, waving to them with a warm smile.

The women exchanged greetings as Jayde and Eleanor rose, ready to part ways once more. There was a bittersweet quality to these goodbyes, each one a reminder of time's fleeting nature.

"You'll begin again," Eleanor said, her voice imbued with the wisdom of a life well-lived. Her eyes twinkled with a mix of mischief and deep understanding. "You'll end again—many times. You'll have many books and stories in your life, too."

Jayde's heart swelled with gratitude. At that moment, she felt the full weight of Eleanor's impact on her life. "I hope so," she replied, her voice thick with emotion. Gathering her courage, she continued, "Eleanor... thank you for being my Soul Helper."

Eleanor's brow furrowed in confusion. "What's that?" she asked, her curiosity evident.

"I read somewhere it's someone who comes into your life for a moment, a lifetime, or anywhere in between and helps your soul grow, heal, and align," Jayde explained, her words resonating with deep personal truth.

A blush crept up Eleanor's cheeks as she looked away, overwhelmed by the sentiment. Jayde smiled, guiding her friend to Charlotte's waiting car.

As Jayde helped Eleanor settle into her seat, the older woman's eyes sparkled with mischief. "Anyway, what about YOUR travels?" she asked, changing the subject. "If you go to Italy, you must stop by the Arno River for me."

"I promise," Jayde said, closing the car door with a soft thud.

Charlotte and Eleanor waved as the car pulled away, leaving Jayde standing on the street, watching until they disappeared from view. A car honked nearby, but Jayde barely noticed, lost in her thoughts.

The park seemed different now, quieter somehow. Jayde took a deep breath, inhaling the scent of autumn leaves and distant possibilities. She felt as if she were standing on the threshold of something new—exciting and terrifying in equal measure.

As she walked back to her own car, Jayde's mind raced with thoughts of the future. Eleanor's words echoed in her mind: "You'll begin again. You'll end again—many times." She wondered what new beginnings awaited her and what stories were yet to be written.

The next few months passed in a whirlwind of activity. Jayde threw herself into her work, meticulously finishing Eleanor's memoir. With each word she typed and every edit she made, she felt increasingly connected to the remarkable woman who had shared her story.

When the book was finally published, Jayde held the first copy in her hands, awestruck by the tangible result of her labor. The cover was simple yet elegant, featuring a black-and-white photograph of Eleanor in her youth, her eyes bright with promise. The title, The Force of the Wind, perfectly captured the essence of Eleanor's indomitable spirit.

As the book gained traction, Jayde found herself swept up in a flurry of interviews and book signings. She spoke passionately about Eleanor's life, sharing the wisdom gleaned from their conversations. With each retelling, the story seemed to take on a life of its own, touching hearts and minds far beyond what she had ever imagined.

Yet during this time, Jayde felt a restlessness growing inside her. Eleanor's tales of Italy had planted a seed, and now that seed was beginning to sprout. The idea of visiting the places Eleanor had described, of walking the same streets and breathing the same air, became an irresistible pull.

Four months later, Jayde found herself standing at the juncture of the Ponte Vecchio bridge and the Arno River in Florence, Italy. The night air was cool against her skin, carrying the scents of the ancient city—stone, water, and a hint of distant cuisine.

The Arno flowed beneath her feet, its waters dark and mysterious in the dim light. Jayde leaned against the stone railing of the bridge, feeling the weight of centuries beneath her hands. She took a deep breath, closing her eyes to savor the moment.

"I'm finally going to leave the past behind me," she whispered into the night. The words felt right as if she were making a pact with the universe.

Jayde looked down at the water, watching the play of light on its surface. A chuckle escaped her lips as a memory surfaced. "Spilled milk and all," she murmured, recalling an old conversation with Eleanor.

"What's a river got to do with milk?" a familiar voice asked from behind her.

Startled, Jayde spun around to find Thani standing there, his expression unreadable. The sight of him sent a jolt through her, a mix of surprise, joy, and nervousness.

"Thani!" Jayde exclaimed, her heart leaping. "Are you here on vacation too?"

Thani shook his head, a small smile tugging at his lips. "Not exactly," he said, holding up a book.

Jayde's eyes widened as she recognized the cover: The Force of the Wind: A Memoir by Eleanor Russo as Dictated to Jayde Masipang-Rivera. She took the book from him, her hands steady despite the rush of emotions.

"You bought my book," Jayde whispered, awe and gratitude mingling in her voice. She looked up at Thani, searching his face for understanding—or perhaps approval.

Thani shrugged, his smile widening slightly. "I wanted to know what was so important about the woman you always met with."

They stood in silence for a moment, their shared history pulling them closer. The sounds of the city faded away, leaving only the gentle lapping of the river and the quiet beating of their hearts.

"But why are you here, and how did you find me at this very moment?" Jayde asked, her voice barely above a whisper. She hardly dared to hope.

Thani's smile grew. "Apparently, I know you better than you know yourself."

"I've always thought you were psychic," Jayde teased, slipping back into their familiar banter.

"Oh? Maybe we're soulmates," Thani countered, his eyes twinkling with mirth.

Jayde laughed, shaking her head. "Felipe told you."

"Yeah, he did," Thani admitted, chuckling.

The laughter faded, replaced by a more serious tone. Jayde felt her unspoken words of apologies were long overdue. "I don't think I'm superior," she said softly, meeting Thani's gaze.

"I know," Thani replied equally gently.

Another moment of silence passed between them.

"I'm really sorry for everything I said," Jayde confessed, her heart in her throat.

"I know," Thani said simply.

He took a step closer, his eyes never leaving hers. "I did miss you, believe it or not."

Jayde gestured around them, a smile playing on her lips. "I know."

As they stood there, smiling at each other, a gentle breeze swirled around them, carrying the promise of new beginnings. The air felt charged with possibility, the potential for something beautiful to bloom from the ashes of their past.

Unable to hold back, Jayde ran to Thani, throwing her arms around him in a fierce hug. Thani staggered back, surprised by the sudden display of affection.

The book fell from Jayde's hands, but she paid no mind to it. As Thani reached for it, Jayde pulled him close, capturing his lips in a passionate kiss. After a moment's hesitation, Thani melted into the embrace, releasing the pent-up feelings he'd held back for so long.

When they finally broke apart, both slightly breathless, Jayde rested her forehead against Thani's. "I can't believe you're here," she murmured, her voice filled with wonder.

Thani chuckled softly, his breath warm against her skin. "I couldn't let you face Italy alone," he teased, though his eyes were serious. "Besides, I had a feeling you might need this." He reached into his jacket and pulled out a small, weathered notebook.

Jayde gasped as she recognized it—Eleanor's old travel journal, the one she had mentioned wanting to retrace. "How did you...?"

"Eleanor gave it to me before I left," Thani explained with a soft smile. "She said you might need a guide."

Tears pricked at Jayde's eyes as she took the journal, overwhelmed by the thoughtfulness of both Eleanor and Thani. "She knew," Jayde whispered, more to herself than to him. "Somehow, she knew."

Thani nodded, his expression tender. "She's a remarkable woman," he said softly. "I can see why she means so much to you."

Jayde looked up at him, her heart full to bursting. "Thank you," she said, pouring all her gratitude into those two simple words. "For being here, for understanding, for... everything."

Thani responded by pulling her close again, pressing a gentle kiss to her forehead. "Always," he murmured against her skin.

As they stood there, wrapped in each other's arms with the lights of Florence twinkling around them, Jayde felt a sense of peace settle over her. The past, with all its regrets and missed opportunities, seemed to fade away. Here, in this moment, was the promise of a new beginning—a new story waiting to be written.

Miles away, in the quiet of her room at Nerine Assisted Living, Eleanor lay peacefully in bed, the final page of the memoir open before her. The soft glow of her bedside lamp cast a warm light over the room, illuminating the array of photographs and mementos that adorned her walls and shelves.

Eleanor's eyes, though tired, sparkled with satisfaction as she read the last few lines. With a contented smile, she closed the book and placed it gently on her nightstand.

As she settled under the covers, her gaze drifted to the wedding portrait of her and Emilio, now holding a place of honor beside her. Reaching out, she tenderly traced the outline of his face.

"Goodnight, Emilio," she whispered, her voice filled with love. "See you soon, my dear."

With those final words, Eleanor's hand fell softly to her side, and her journey in this life came to a peaceful end.

As Eleanor's story concluded, new chapters began. In Florence, Jayde and Thani walked hand in hand along the banks of the Arno, their laughter blending with the timeless sounds of the ancient city. All around the world, readers opened Eleanor's memoir, eager to be inspired by her indomitable spirit and zest for life.

For in the end, that is the power of stories—they live on long after we are gone, touching hearts and changing lives in ways we can never fully comprehend. Eleanor understood this, as did Jayde.

And now, as one journey ended and another began, the cycle of life and love continues, as eternal and unstoppable as the flow of the Arno itself.

Also by Ann Marie Spencer

Your Duende
Wind Shear: A Novella

About the Author

Nomad in spirit preferring rainy days for superb lovemaking, wine drinking and savoring decadent foods.

I live to explore new places and engage in new experiences. Believing that life should be lived to the fullest.

A pessimist yet always hopeful because what else is there to be.

I am a living novel as are we all.

Milton Keynes UK
Ingram Content Group UK Ltd.
UKHW031155251124
451529UK00001B/36